HALFBACK ON HIS OWN

JACKSON SCHOLZ

Halfback on His Own

WILLIAM MORROW & COMPANY

New York, 1962

HALFBACK ON HIS OWN

CHAPTER

1

THE effigy hung high. It dangled grotesquely in the Florida sunshine, a grisly object in the public eye, a cruel and senseless protest by the kind of people who prefer, of course, to remain anonymous.

It was easy enough for those familiar with the football situation at Gulf University to identify the person whom the dummy was supposed to represent. To eliminate all doubt, however, the creators of the effigy had fastened a sign on the dummy's chest—*Judd Hagerty*. Judd Hagerty was head coach of the Pelicans.

The gag, or prank, or outrage, whichever term best suited it, had been carried out spectacularly. The approach to the Administration Building led through a long lane of royal palms, majestic giants with their tall trunks and feathered crowns. A rope had been stretched across the center of the lane from one palm to another. The effigy dangled from the middle of the rope, some thirty feet off the ground. It was a tidy engineering feat, which posed a problem for the removal of the

ugly object. Students on their way to morning classes
stopped to stare. There would be a lot of tardy marks
chalked up today.

Andy Baker would be tardy too. He joined the growing crowd, staring upward with the rest, held there
by the creepy fascination that controlled each new arrival. It seemed to Andy that disapproval was considerably stronger than approval among the students. For
the most part, they were dismayed and angry at the
desecration of their campus, and more particularly,
Andy hoped, at the feeling which had prompted this
display of boorishness.

There were some, however, who seemed to think the
effigy was timely and appropriate. A disturbing number
fell into this class as Andy's eyes swept cautiously across
the crowd. Amused expressions and sly grins told their
story. There were those who believed Judd Hagerty
was getting just what he deserved.

There was usually a small line of worry between
Andy's eyebrows, giving his angular face an air of stu-
dious concern. The line was deeper at the moment,
and his eyes, a smoky blue, were somber. Common
sense told him to leave the crowd and go to class, but
curiosity held him to the spot. Someone announced
that the fire department had been summoned.

Andy decided that the present situation was much
more serious than an impulsive adolescent urge to hang
a football coach in effigy. Exhibitions of this sort normally took place toward the end of a losing season,
spurred by hotheads with too few brains and too much

time on their hands. The difference in this instance was that the first practice session on the home field was scheduled for this same afternoon. The effigy boys appeared to be jumping the gun, an indication that the previous losing season was still fresh in their minds, a great deal fresher than it should have been after a summer away from school.

It all boiled down to the fact that the effigy-minded trouble makers had not been permitted to forget the bad showing of the Pelicans the year before. Pre-season football news appearing in the newspapers had played up the point that a few of the more powerful Gulf alumni were howling for Judd Hagerty's scalp, a condition which had probably prodded the effigy hangers into action. Hagerty and his Pelicans were being sabotaged before they had a chance to start. The alumni were behind it. Andy felt a sickness creeping through him. The most powerful alumnus of them all was Andy's dad.

This much was common knowledge, yet Andy, to this point, felt that the members of the student body had not associated him too closely with the energetic efforts of his father to promote a winning football team. Andy had realized during his freshman year that he was bound to be conspicuous because of his father's fame, and for this reason he had tried to make himself as inconspicuous as possible. He had gained the reputation of a quiet, likable guy who minded his own business and made no attempt to cash in on his dad's importance.

He began to wonder anxiously if the present out-burst would change things for him. It had been un-questionably triggered by a group of meddling alumni, and no one could doubt that Andy's dad was up to his neck in the affair.

He let his eyes move cautiously about the crowd again, hoping his imagination was playing tricks on him. It appeared, though, that too many faces were turned in his direction, that too many eyes were study-ing him with curious interest, wondering what thoughts were rushing through his mind as the effigy above swayed gently in the morning breeze.

He held his face as expressionless as possible, wish-ing he had kept on walking toward his history class. An abrupt departure now would focus more attention on him, and he did not want attention. He might have weathered the ordeal without too much embarrassment except for the arrival of Mark Sutton.

Andy fought down a quiver of apprehension as he saw Mark join the crowd. Mark was a big man with a boisterous self-assurance that too often carried a false note. He was handsome in a heavy-featured sort of way, preferring clothes of positive colors, which would draw eyes in his direction. He was wearing maroon slacks and a canary yellow sport shirt. His hair was strictly Hollywood—abundant, with defined sideburns.

Mark Sutton seemed to feel he had good reason for disliking Andy, even though the reason, to Andy's way of thinking, was absurd. The fathers of both men were television stars, and Andy's dad had a higher TV rating than Mark's dad. The two fathers had been feuding now for several years, with a hostility fostered by the jealousies of the entertainment world. Andy had sensed the friction early in his freshman year and promptly made every effort to avoid Mark, yet give him no chance to indulge a foolish grudge. It now appeared that Mark might have his chance, and he was just the sort of guy to take advantage of it. His face lit up when he spotted Andy. Instead of moving closer he chose to let his loud voice bridge the distance.

"Hey, Andy! What do you think of that cute little job up there above you?"

If Mark's purpose was to gain attention, he succeeded. The crowd stopped its excited chattering, letting the silence close in solidly while all eyes turned toward Andy. Andy felt the hot blood creeping into his face and hated himself because he couldn't prevent it. It might easily be assumed by the people nearest him that his color was a sign of shame instead of anger. He even battled with the swift, disturbing thought that a portion of the color *might* be caused by shame.

While he was trying hard to form some sort of answer, Mark cut loose again. "Can't you think of anybody, Andy, who might want Judd Hagerty to lose his job?"

The affair was getting sticky. Much as Andy hated a messy business like this, he found his anger pushing hard against its safety valve. Whatever might have happened at this stage, however, was left to guesswork, for the arrival of a newcomer spared him the hard choice of tangling with Mark Sutton or backing away from an unpleasant situation.

Andy first became aware of the diversion when a small shock wave traveled through the crowd. The warning mutter from a student spread the tremor swiftly, whipping all eyes toward the new center of attention. Judd Hagerty was about to join the gathering.

He moved with the slow deliberation of a person with a lot of time to spare, a block of a man, square and powerful, still capable in his middle age of demonstrating the sort of line play he expected from his gridiron pupils. His eyes, an intense blue, could convey a sudden chill if the occasion called for it. At the moment they were mild and calm, in spite of the circumstances.

His unexpected presence caught the students flat-footed. In an exchange of apprehensive glances they were asking one another what the book of etiquette suggested under these conditions. It was impossible to ignore Judd Hagerty, yet no one seemed inclined to discuss the matter of the effigy with him. There were a few muttered phrases which, sounding too much like condolences to a bereaved relative, soon trickled off to join the silence.

In other words, Judd Hagerty was giving the effigy watchers a bad time. He glanced at no one, spoke to no one. He ignored the effigy. He leaned, relaxed, against one of the trees to which the rope was tied. After filling his pipe from a tobacco pouch with slow deliberation, he lighted it with steady fingers, expelling the smoke in the thoughtful manner of a head coach mapping football strategy.

It was a shrewd and calculated bit of drama which Judd Hagerty probably hoped would serve a double purpose. He had recognized the presence of the effigy simply by the act of appearing on the scene, yet by his calm indifference he was setting an example of how the gag should be regarded. He had also proved that he considered being hung in effigy no disgrace—nothing sufficiently important to make him blow his top or hide his shame from public view. He was placing himself promptly on display, leaving the next move up to those who seemed to think the effigy was a big enough attraction to stop traffic.

No one, however, seemed inclined to make a move. Andy knew exactly how the others felt, because he felt that way himself, wishing he were anywhere but right here in the disturbing presence of Judd Hagerty. He heard the subdued shuffling of feet and the occasional nervous clearing of a throat. The watchers soon began to drift away, trying, but not succeeding, to make their retreat look casual as they left the battlefield to Hagerty. Andy joined the movement, trying not to slink. He heard the siren of the fire truck on its way, with ladders long enough to reach the effigy.

Some of Andy's uneasiness wore off as he resumed his walk toward class, but the unsettling memory of Mark Sutton still disturbed him. The encounter had not been pleasant, yet Andy realized that it had been inevitable.

Andy's father, Jocko Baker, was, by grace of public fancy, the top-rated comedian in the country. Mark's dad, Tex Sutton, was a western star who took it pretty hard when Jocko Baker's program moved ahead of his in national rating. Tex thereupon, according to the quotes, tabbed Jocko as a slobbering buffoon, and Jocko countered with the pleasantry that Tex rode horseback like a stuffed ape, and couldn't draw his six-gun fast enough to shoot a turtle. There was more of the same as time went on, leaving a nation-wide impression that Tex and Jocko did not love each other.

The whole thing seemed ridiculous to Andy. Mark took a different view of it, feeling, obviously, that conditions warranted a second generation feud even if it had to be one-sided. He may also have believed he was being loyal to his dad, but Andy's private theory was that Mark had inherited his father's urge to be a public figure, and was not too particular as to how he gained attention. It was easy enough, therefore, for Mark to associate himself with the Baker-Sutton feud, and to draw a bead on the clay pigeon, Andy Baker.

The situation promised to get worse. To this point Mark's and Andy's paths had not crossed other than by chance. It would be different now. Mark Sutton was good football material, a promising sophomore upon whom the coaches were depending to add strength to the Pelican backfield. Andy was going to find out soon how good a player he was. He would report this afternoon for his first workout with the Pelicans.

CHAPTER

2

GULF University was situated on the Florida west coast near St. Petersburg. Its setting provided a sweeping view of Tampa Bay, which joined the Gulf of Mexico almost at the university's doorstep. The Sunshine Skyway, bridging the bay, was visible in the distance, its graceful span arching high above the water.

The buildings of the university, though strongly built against the threat of hurricanes, were designed for beauty, their cool green stucco blending skillfully with tropical trees, vines, and shrubbery. Utility and convenience had not been neglected. With the aid of modern science, Gulf enjoyed the best of everything, including a small yacht basin where the boats of students could be moored. The university could well afford such luxuries. It was never cramped for funds.

Gulf's registration was limited to approximately five thousand students. The university held a unique place among schools of comparable size, due largely to the background of so many of its undergraduates. It made no effort to solicit sons and daughters of parents in the entertainment world, yet the trend was definitely in that direction. It had been going on for some time now, removing the trend from the category of a fad.

Andy's father might have been responsible for this to some extent. Andy had been exposed to the entertainment world long enough to recognize a sheeplike quality in members of the profession, a compelling urge to follow the lead of entertainers who had made the grade.

Jocko Baker had made the grade. Since being graduated from Gulf he had sponsored the school with an almost fanatic zeal. If it needed money Jocko shelled out lavishly. It was believed he might have done so even if such gifts were not exempt from federal tax. He was, quite naturally, chairman of the university's board of directors, in which position he swung formidable weight.

Andy had had no choice of schools. It had to be Gulf University or war in the family, and Andy had no urge to battle with his dad. Small uprisings in the past had been overridden easily by Jocko's grand, expansive manner, by his complete assurance that he knew all the answers. There was little father-and-son closeness between the pair, yet since the death of Andy's mother many years ago, Andy admitted grudgingly that Jocko, in his way, had done the best he could. He had not remarried. This much, Andy felt, was to his father's credit.

Andy's freshman year had been somewhat of an ordeal, and he had acquired a grim, deep-seated urge to claw his way from beneath the smothering weight of his father's reputation. It would not be easy. To accomplish the big job he would have to make a sizable splash of some sort in the campus life, and the equipment he possessed for such a splash was not encouraging. Football? It was the only thing in which he dared place much hope.

He loved football. So much on the optimistic side. Unfortunately, his love for football had not distinguished him on the prep-school gridiron. He had tried as hard as anyone, but he simply lacked the weight and the co-ordination. He had never been entirely sure of what his hands and feet might do.

He was encouraged now, however, by his added weight. During the past year his big-boned frame had furnished ample room for an extra twenty pounds, bringing the total to one hundred and eighty-five. Most of his adolescent awkwardness had vanished, permitting him to move with greater confidence, assured now that his muscles would obey the commands of his brain and that his feet would not get tangled at improper times.

He had not, unfortunately, been able to give his new ability the football test. The Pelicans, with the help of the alumni, recruited football talent as aggressively as any other school, but the alumni, to this point, had lost a major battle with the members of the faculty who controlled the academic standard of the school. A football player had to keep his grades up or he got the ax.

It did not matter if he could tote the pigskin through a pack of wild gorillas, he had to keep his grades up.

The rule, quite sensibly, applied to freshmen too, a rule which Andy ran into head on. His first-year grades, though not disastrous, were shaky enough to keep him out of freshman football. It was a bitter disappointment, for which Andy blamed no one but himself. Normally a good student, he had found it hard to concentrate on books during the early months of school. He had been too involved with the emotional problem of adjusting himself to the public role of Jocko Baker's son in a school where Jocko Baker was so well-known. By the time his academic grades began to climb, it was too late for football.

He tried to console himself with the belief that everything had worked out for the best, that his added weight and improved co-ordination would permit him to make a better showing on the football field. The fact remained, however, that he had missed a valuable year of coaching and experience, and that the question of his real ability, if any, was still unanswered.

His thoughts kept moving toward his first football workout that afternoon. It was just as well for Andy that all classroom procedure on the opening day was brief, concerned mostly with roll calls and study assignments for the following day. It would have been hard for him to concentrate upon a lecture.

It was too early for football practice by the time he left his final class. He started for his dormitory room, one of the few things in which he could take pride since

entering the university. He had bucked his dad for
the privilege of living in a dormitory, a feat that, in
itself, had taken lots of guts. Jocko, though outraged,
had finally given in, accepting the compromise that
Andy would consider joining a fraternity once he had
had a chance to settle down in college life.

The fraternities had battled like a pack of wild dogs,
whipping themselves into a frenzy for the distinction
of pledging Andy Baker; and Andy, far from flattered,
was pretty well soured, temporarily at least, at the idea
of becoming a Greek letter man. He was smart enough
to know that each fraternity was trying to grab off
Jocko Baker's son and would have welcomed an Af-
rican Bushman into the fold under similar conditions.

Andy did not reject the thought of joining a fraternity at some later date, but when that time came he
would have to be completely sure they wanted *him,*
instead of Jocko Baker's son. Jocko took it pretty hard
that Andy even refused to hook up with the fraternity
to which Jocko himself belonged, but Andy stuck to
his guns. He checked in at a dormitory, and up to this
point he had not regretted it.

There was nothing wrong with Gulf's dormitories.
They were modern and attractive. The lobbies were as
fine as those of any first-class hotel, and there were
spacious rooms with private baths for those who could
afford it. Andy could afford it. His father might have
had some faults, but stinginess was not among them,
particularly with regard to Andy, who owned his own
imported sport car and a small, fast cabin cruiser.

The boat was in recognition of Andy's great love for skin diving, a sport which he had enjoyed for several years. It was important to Jocko Baker that his son should skin dive in style. It was Jocko's way of acting like a father, a thing which Andy understood, even though it saddened him at times to realize that his dad and he were virtually strangers. He accepted Jocko's indulgence with the casual gratitude of a person who has been accustomed all his life to wealth. It neither turned his head nor made him feel more important than his fellow students.

Andy's room was on the third floor, with a restful view of Tampa Bay. He had left the elevator and was rounding a corner in the corridor when he collided violently with someone coming from the opposite direction. The impact was considerable, and though Andy was no lightweight, he got by far the worst of it. He had the startled impression of barging into some huge animal the size of a horse, but quickly saw that the animal was not quite as big.

Andy bounced back, regained his breath, and took a better look. The man was big by any standard. He looked ponderously fat, yet Andy had encountered no softness in the meeting. Surprise showed briefly in his eyes.

"I'm sorry!" blurted the big man, sounding as if he really meant it.

"No harm done," said Andy. Then, "You're Sam Tedder, aren't you? I've seen you around the campus."

"Yes, I'm Tedder," he admitted, adding without

boastfulness, "I guess I'm really conspicuous. They say I block out a lot of scenery. You're Andy Baker."

Andy's face went involuntarily tight. It was habit by this time, a quick defense against the approach of any stranger, most of whom wanted a closer look and probably a few words with Jocko Baker's son.

The moment was not improved when Sam said in his mild high-pitched voice, so out of keeping with his size, "I didn't think it would happen in just this way, but I've sure been wanting to meet you."

Andy froze a little tighter. He told himself, "Well, here it comes," anything from an autograph request to a run-down of his dad's eating habits. Some of Jocko's admirers even believed themselves capable of writing part of Jocko's gag material, a deal which would, of course, be arranged by Andy.

So Andy braced himself, determined to follow his usual policy of being as polite as possible, which wasn't always easy. He was not prepared, however, for Sam's immediate reaction. A gentle, look of compassion showed in Sam's brown eyes. He made a clucking noise denoting pity.

"You've got it real bad, haven't you?" said Sam.

Andy, caught off balance, replied faintly, "Got what bad?"

"A Jocko Baker complex."

Andy's first impulse was to tell the other to mind his own business, but there was something oddly reassuring in the big man's attitude, the air of a person who was trespassing with the kindliest of motives. Andy was surprised to find his indignation fading. He was even more surprised by the feeling that he owed Sam an apology.

He heard himself saying, "I—I'm sorry, Sam."

"Thanks for the vote of confidence," Sam acknowledged soberly. "I told you I've been wanting to meet you, and that's the truth. The point is, it has nothing at all to do with your dad. I only wanted to talk about skin diving."

It was Andy's turn to brighten. "Well, fine!" he said impulsively. "Let's talk about it in my room."

"Lead on," said Sam.

In the short walk to Andy's door he began to wonder what was happening to him. He had just issued a reckless invitation out of keeping with his policy of protecting his own privacy. Sam Tedder, it is true, had touched a soft spot when he had mentioned skin diving. Andy knew that he liked this mountain of a man in a way he had not permitted himself to like another man since he had entered Gulf.

Once in the room Andy seated himself in a deep chair and motioned Sam toward another. The position of the chair did not suit Sam so he moved it to another spot, lifting the heavy piece of furniture as if it were made of balsa wood. He answered Andy's startled expression of disbelief.

"It's not all fat," said Sam almost apologetically. "It just looks that way. I'm pretty strong."

"My gosh, you must be," said Andy, slightly awed. "Judd Hagerty could use you in that line."

"That's what he says," admitted Sam. "But he's pretty peeved with me right now. I came here on a football scholarship but almost flunked out my freshman year, so they wouldn't let me play. When it finally sank in that I wasn't down here on a vacation, I kept my nose in the books for a few months and boosted my grades enough to make me eligible this year. The coach has begun speaking to me again, and I'm going to the workout this afternoon." He considered Andy's build and general look of ruggedness before asking, "Are you a football man?"

"I honestly don't know," said Andy. He answered Sam's puzzled look by explaining the situation. "I'm going to give it a whirl, though, and I guess it won't take long to find out whether or not I've got the stuff."

"I think you'll have it," Sam said promptly.

It was Andy's turn to be puzzled. "Why do you think so?"

"Well," said Sam carefully, "you'll be starting off with an incentive that the rest of us don't have, something that'll drive you mighty hard."

Andy stared at Sam, finding it hard to believe that Sam, on such brief acquaintance, had put a finger on the sensitive area of Andy's problem.

Sam eliminated any doubt by saying apologetically, "It's none of my business, Andy, but I happen to be the sort of guy who likes to know what makes the wheels go round in other people. In your case it's pretty obvious you've let yourself be overshadowed by your dad, and it's mighty important to you to begin

casting a shadow of your own. You may find the chance
in football. That's what I mean by saying you'll have
more incentive than a lot of other guys."

Andy shrugged acceptance of Sam's statement. "I
hope you're right."

"I hope I am too. Now, how about this scuba stuff?"

"How did you know I was a scuba fan?" asked Andy
curiously.

"I go down to the yacht basin now and then. I've
seen your boat and I've talked to guys. I hear you're a
fine diver."

They changed the subject from football to skin diving. Sam Tedder seemed to be a real fan, and to know
a lot about the sport. Andy cautiously withheld judgment, though, knowing that many people can be skin-
diving enthusiasts above the water, but once beneath
the surface, may easily ignore many of the fundamentals. Sam said he had his own scuba gear, yet here again
there were scuba gears and scuba gears. Inadequate or
cheap equipment was an invitation to disaster.

"Have you joined the Dolphins?" asked Andy. The
Dolphins was a scuba club made up of university students.

Sam shook his head. "Too busy studying. I hope to
join it this year. Are you a member?"

"Yes. But—well, I'm afraid I haven't been too so-
ciable about it." He glanced at his watch, announcing,
"Looks like it's about time for football. We better get
over there."

He arose from his chair, trying to appear casual as

if football practice was merely a routine. His insides began to churn, however, as they headed for the Athletic Center. He was finding it hard to draw his breath in normally. He was eager, and at the same time definitely scared. He was heading toward one of the big adventures of his life.

CHAPTER

3

THE Athletic Center was in keeping with the other things about Gulf University—no money spared. The buildings formed a huge rectangle. The Administration Building with its big-business set-up, stretched across the front. The swimming pool, with a roof which could be mechanically rolled back, took up one end. The gymnasium and the field house formed the other sides.

The enclosed rectangle had been made into a park or, more precisely, into a small domain ruled by a bad-tempered tyrant known as Mike. Mike was a pelican, the official mascot, and no one was more aware of his official privileges than Mike himself. He was a bully and a snob, despite which he demanded and received respect from everyone.

He swam majestically in the small pond in the center of the park or dozed upon the bank. There was no need to post *Keep Off the Grass* signs, because Mike was the self-appointed guardian of the turf. Visitors could walk safely on the paths of white crushed shell, but found it risky to attempt short cuts because Mike was seldom as sleepy as he appeared to be. He could move with speed and stealth, specializing in rear assaults, and the sharp hook at the end of his long beak could properly be described as a lethal weapon. Whenever a yell of pain came from the park, everyone knew what had happened.

Mike made occasional brief trips into the outer world to associate with his own kind, but would tolerate no return calls from his friends. He had a fine racket going here with all the free fish he could eat. There was no need for him to make those headlong, body-jarring dives for food. He could get all he wanted here at home without batting his brains out in the process.

Mike was required, however, to perform a service for these privileges, a service which outraged and mortified him. He had to be present at the football games, a duty he accepted with bad grace. It was necessary, of course, to tie him to his perch with a short length of cord, and, after a few humiliating nose dives, he was smart enough to know he had to stay there. He hated football. He watched the games with sullen scorn.

Mike was on duty in the park when Sam and Andy crossed from the Administration Building to the gym. They had enrolled at the receiving office where they had been given cards which would permit them to check out uniforms. Both men, nervous and preoccupied with football, took a short cut across the grass.

Andy was first to recognize the blunder. He let out a sharp yell of warning as Mike went into action.

Mike, to give him credit, did not have a yellow feather on his spine. Without hesitation he selected the more formidable foe, hurling himself at Sam Tedder's bulk. Sam, however, surprised both Mike and Andy by his sudden burst of speed. Mike made a game try, but his wicked beak snapped shut a full inch from the seat of Sam's pants.

Andy, meanwhile, had managed to get his own feet slightly tangled and was still vulnerable by the time Sam reached the safety of the path. Mike, humiliated by his poor showing, decided not to let it happen again. It was Andy's turn, and Andy, knowing he had no chance to reach the path in time, was determined not to present Mike with his favorite target.

Andy also used his head in the emergency, reasoning that, by facing his attacker, he might be able to parry Mike's thrust with a slap of his hand. He was crouched and ready for the onslaught when a strange thing happened. Mike skidded to a halt within arm's length of Andy's last-ditch stand. Mike cocked his head and regarded Andy with an accusing eye, plainly suggesting that Andy had spoiled his fun and that Mike was not accustomed to this sort of treatment. Andy, for some unaccountable reason, held his ground.

It was a strange tableau, tense enough to lack amusement at the moment, as man and bird tried to stare each other down. There was no way of knowing what went on in the small area Mike used for a brain. He may have been respecting Andy's courage, or he may have been suffering a bewilderment he could not cope with. At any rate, he finally ducked his head with the embarrassed gesture of a kid caught stealing cookies, and Andy, obeying a swift impulse, reached out a hand and scratched the top of Mike's head.

Andy was still taut, ready to snatch his hand back any instant, a precaution which proved unnecessary. Mike seemed to like the scratching process. He even moved in a little closer to encourage more of it. His attitude seemed to say, "I'm probably making a big fool of myself. So what? I like this guy."

Sam, watching with amazement, said, "Now I've seen everything."

"So have I," admitted Andy.

"Are you sure none of your ancestors were pelicans?" asked Sam.

"I've spent so much time under water," Andy said with a grin, "that maybe Mike thinks I've got a pocket full of fish."

He backed carefully away. The two men started for the gym keeping a cautious eye to the rear. Mike followed peacefully, making small noises of protest as he waddled. He escorted them to the door.

Andy turned and said, "So long, Mike. See you later."

Mike nodded solemnly, assuring Andy he would keep the date.

They made their way to the equipment room, where a long counter separated the football candidates from the tier of bins containing football togs, which ranged from new to badly worn. The room was presided over by Pop Glendon, a job he had handled with gruff efficiency since football became a major sport at Gulf.

His face was lined and his eyes were bright and sharp under beetling white brows. He not only knew his stock, but had a sound working knowledge of the men who wore the uniforms he handed out. He knew their relative importance as football players, and this was apt to influence his decision on how good their uniforms should be. Sam and Andy held red slips in their hands, indicating that they were first-year men who would be trying for positions on the varsity.

He spotted Sam at once. "Huh," he grunted testily. "Sam Tedder. You almost turned out to be a poor investment."

"Almost," agreed Sam cheerfully.

Pop scowled and said, "So I'm supposed to find an outfit for a hippopotamus. We're fresh out of circus tents."

"Shucks, Pop," said Sam good-naturedly, "just give me two of everything. I'll make out."

Pop's lips moved slightly at the corners, indicating that he liked to have his little jokes appreciated. "No kidding, Sam," he said. "You've put me on the spot. I'll do the best I can, though, until I can order something that'll fit you."

He gave Sam the biggest uniform he had in stock, before turning his attention to Andy. A quick glance told him Andy's size together with the fact that he was neither a recruited player nor one who had shown promise during his freshman year—in other words, a football nobody. Pop started down the line toward the used uniform department. He stopped suddenly, whirled, and took a double take.

"Oh-oh," he said, in the manner of a man who has almost made a serious blunder. He returned to another bin, from which he handed Andy a brand-new uniform.

"What's the idea?" demanded Andy, promptly wishing he had kept his mouth shut. By this time several other football men had entered the equipment room.

"I didn't recognize you right away," said Pop, as if it explained everything.

Andy felt the blood surging to his face, wishing again he had held his tongue. Once involved, however, he was not the sort to back away. He asked, "What difference does it make? You know I don't rate a new uniform."

"It's a matter of opinion," Pop said quietly. "And in this case I think my opinion is better than yours."

"But *why?*" Andy burst out helplessly.

"Now look, son," Pop said patiently. "I know my job and I'm not scared of losing it. In this deal I'm just being practical. If you don't blossom out in a new outfit it'll be only a short time before I have to give you one anyway, and it probably won't have anything to do with your brand of football."

"But I don't rate a new uniform," repeated Andy, getting in deeper.

"You may not think so, son," Pop said, "and *I* might

not think so. In fact, a lot of people might not think
so. The fact remains that certain people *will* think so,
and those are the ones I've got to outguess right here in
this room. Do you follow me?"

"I'm afraid I do," said Andy uncomfortably. "And—
and thanks."

"It's okay, kid," said Pop. "Just take it easy."

Andy gathered up his gear and hurried from the
room. Angry and embarrassed, he refused to meet the
eyes of the men waiting for their outfits. They had had
an earful, and Andy did not care to know what they
were thinking.

On the way to the locker room, Andy asked bitterly,
"Is this the way it's going to be?"

He was asking the question of himself, scarcely aware
he had spoken aloud. Sam recognized this probably,
but decided to answer it just the same.

"I think not," he said slowly. "I can see Pop's side of
it, but Pop doesn't happen to coach the football team.
If you've got any worries about being a fair-haired boy
once you get out on the field, I think you can forget
them. Judd Hagerty doesn't scare, and he thinks in
terms of football. He can be a nice guy or a tough one
if he has to. You won't get any breaks from him."

Andy let his breath out gustily. "I've let my brain
get twisted up," he admitted, "and it's time I began
untwisting it. Maybe I can play college football and
maybe I can't. I'll never find out, though, until I quit
worrying about what people think."

"You can get yourself real fouled up," conceded Sam,

"with worries of that sort." He paused a minute before saying, "Football's mighty important to you, isn't it?"

"I doubt if you could guess how important it really is."

Sam said quietly, "I think I could."

Andy shot him a swift look, suddenly convinced that the big man understood his problem, even on such short acquaintance.

The locker room was spacious, airy, and well lighted. One of the assistant student football managers met them there and assigned them to adjoining lockers. The room began to fill with husky football men before Andy and Sam had finished dressing. The regulars, men who had proved themselves varsity material, were not accorded the distinction of an area to themselves. It was Judd Hagerty's policy to scatter the lockers of the newcomers among those of the experienced men, making close association almost unavoidable. The practice was primarily designed to show recruits that Hagerty played no favorites. It also served to encourage friendships and a closer unity between the old-timers and the hopefuls.

Andy, while dressing, kept his eyes strictly on his work, realizing that his bright new outfit stood out in sharp contrast to second-hand uniforms being donned by some of the other sophomores. Andy had tensed himself, waiting to hear some comment on the matter, but when the comment came he found his preparations were inadequate. He could not subdue a surge of apprehension.

A voice said, "Since when have they been handing

out new gear to guys who weren't even on the freshman squad? There must be a real good reason for it."

Andy recognized the voice at once, Mark Sutton's. Andy had not seen Mark come in, but it appeared now that Mark's locker was across the aisle. Andy checked the urge to whirl around as he swallowed the brassy taste of anger in his throat—an unnatural anger, greater than it should have been. It frightened him a bit to learn that Mark could affect him in this way. He waited for Mark to open up again.

Mark might have intended to if he had had the chance. He found, however, from an unexpected source, that his type of humor was not popular. A gruff voice of authority said, "Knock it off!"

The voice came from Cal Beeker, who was sitting beside Mark on a bench. Cal had not paused in the careful process of lacing his right shoe. He had merely issued an order which he expected to be obeyed, and Cal Beeker, a star tackle for the Pelicans, possessed some two hundred and twenty-five pounds with which to back up such an order.

Mark's mouth closed slowly. His face reddened in admission of defeat, but he had sense enough to know when he was climbing the wrong fence. Even though he had been a bright backfield prospect as a freshman, he was not secure enough to stick his neck out farther at a time like this.

Andy, fully dressed, no longer had an excuse to face his locker. He turned with an effort, forcing his eyes to travel among the other men. There was little to be seen.

Each man was meticulously attending to his own business with a studied indifference that added considerable strain to the situation.

Ding Kibby, a fast thinker in his job at quarterback, broke the tension. "Hey, Sam!" he called. "Who's your tailor?"

The Pelicans welcomed the diversion, shifting their attention promptly to Sam Tedder, who was, indeed, a sight to behold. The jersey fitted Sam like the skin of a toy balloon, giving the impression that a pin prick would be disastrous. The pants, it is true, were meant for a big man, but in order to achieve the proper waist size they reached almost to the ankles of Sam's stocky legs. His round head poked out from the top of his misfitting garments like a basketball balanced on a sack of oats.

"Fetching, isn't it?" said Sam.

He gave them a fashion show. He minced up and down the aisle, turning this way and that with the exaggerated gestures of a mannequin displaying a French-imported evening gown. It was a fine performance. The Pelicans were ready for a laugh, and Sam accommodated them.

When the show was over they started for the field. Andy joined them, trying to make himself as inconspicuous as possible. He was nervous and knew he had every right to be. He had waited a long time for this important moment—the chance to find out, one way or another, whether he was college football caliber.

CHAPTER

4

THE stadium adjoined the Athletic Center. It looked, from the outside, like a huge white frosted cake. The interior was bowl-shaped, capable of seating sixty thousand fans. Floodlight towers had been installed for night games, and the spacious press box was designed to keep the writers comfortable and happy.

The practice area of two complete football fields was behind the stadium. The players were protected from the abrasive qualities of Florida sand by a carpet of fine turf. The practice area had been planted with Bermuda grass, and was tended with the care that a golf fairway at a country club would receive. It was quite a layout.

Some of Andy's self-consciousness evaporated by the time they reached the field and the players had been divided into groups. Sam, because of his impressive high-school record, was promptly spotted in one of the higher echelons. Andy, as was to be expected, found himself in a squad of men with no impressive records.

The majority of these men, Andy sensed, were also

fighting nerves. They were all, with Andy, at the bottom of the pile, all concerned with their own ambitious hopes and doubts. They had no time or inclination to be critical of Andy's uniform. Andy had a strong urge just the same to take the newness from his duds by wallowing on the ground a bit, an urge which was denied fulfillment on this opening day of training.

A rangy individual approached the group, a young man in his late twenties wearing a T-shirt, a baseball cap, and a whistle hanging by a cord about his neck, the unmistakable identification of a coach. He introduced himself as Harry Todd, a name which Andy recognized as that of an all-American end of several years ago.

Todd grinned and said, "Now comes the worst part, calisthenics. I used to hate the routine, and still do. Unfortunately, it's part of football. The harder we get our muscles now, the less chance we have of getting ourselves cracked up later on. Also, it'll give me an early chance to find out what sort of shape you're in. It's easy to put on a little fat during the summer."

He gave them a rough workout. He set them an example, though, vigorously going through each exercise himself, a tacit proof that he was not here to enjoy their misery or to assume the role of slave driver. It was significant that Harry Todd was in better shape than many of the others when he finally gave them a chance to rest.

"See what I mean?" he panted. "Some of you guys are soft as putty. Don't worry, though, I've got the cure for it." He grinned again at the sound of several heart-felt groans.

Andy, to his satisfaction, found he had survived the workout well. He was in better shape than he had hoped, a credit he gave to many hours of swimming. The underwater work had gone far toward developing his breath control. He was not puffing as laboriously as the others. If Coach Todd noticed the difference he made no comment on it.

Todd waited until the men were breathing normally again before announcing, "I've got to know how fast you boys can move. We'll try it at one hundred yards. Line up, and take off when I drop my arm. It may be a little early for this sort of thing, but time is limited."

There was considerable significance to Todd's last statement. The young coach meant that the nineteen men in the squad were more or less expendable, because the chances were very slim that any of them would turn out to be varsity material. Otherwise, they would have been discovered before now. An all-out sprint without previous training could be risky from the standpoint of pulled muscles or strained tendons. The time element, however, made the risk essential.

Efficiency was the keynote in a big football organization, and wasted time was something to be frowned on. The weeding out process of these nineteen men must be accomplished quickly, permitting time to be spent on more important things. Todd obviously had been ordered to single out those, if any, who showed promise, and not to fool around with the job.

Judd Hagerty was an advocate of speed. He wanted plenty of it on offense and defense, and was even willing to sacrifice some weight for speed. With the proper material Hagerty's ground offensive could be awesome, a vanguard of speedy backs and maybe a couple of fast linemen to run interference for the ball carrier, together with split-second timing, could give the opposition lots of headaches.

Andy understood this, and, as a backfield candidate, he knew he had to have the speed. He believed he had it. How much he could only guess. He had done some experimental sprinting along the beach, and had liked the feel of it. In prep school his legs had always wanted to move too fast for his cumbersome feet, giving an unhinged effect to his earnest efforts. Now, however, with his added weight and vastly improved co-ordination, his feet seemed willing to behave. His solo sprints had given him no basis for comparison, but that matter would soon be remedied. There were eighteen other men lined up across the field, each one of whom would put out everything he had.

By the time Todd had paced off the proper distance Andy had worked himself into a fine nervous dither. He was tense as a spring, his eyes glued to Todd's upraised arm.

When the arm flashed downward Andy went into action with a reckless burst which, in his prep-school days, would have sent him flat on his face. He had not intended so rash a gamble. He was happily amazed to find himself still on his feet and running, and even more amazed to find no one in front of him, a situation which did not last long.

He had traveled no more than twenty-five yards when he saw a figure pulling in the lead, a smooth, long-striding man with wings upon his heels. Andy made the blunder, then, of trying to overhaul the man ahead, and it took another twenty-five yards to prove to Andy that he didn't have a chance against the speedster.

By the time this truth bore in upon him, Andy had managed to get himself in trouble. The added effort tied him into knots, and, for a fearful instant, it seemed that some of his prep-school awkwardness had returned. He was surrounded now by pounding feet. His chest began to tighten as quick panic grabbed at him, and the panic brought the help he needed.

It came from an unexpected source—his long training as a skin diver. He had been in a few tight underwater spots, situations where a flood of panic could be deadly. He had learned to control his breathing and his muscles in dangerous moments of this sort. His life was not threatened at the moment, yet the feeling of panic was so similar that he controlled it automatically.

It made a tremendous difference. His legs began to limber and his breath reached down again into the bottom of his lungs. The feeling of awkwardness evaporated. The labored grunts and pounding feet on either side of him were no longer ominous. He did not overhaul the leader, but by keeping his stride as smooth as possible he finished a healthy second.

He felt mighty good about it. It was far from a conclusive proof that he was varsity material or was even fast enough for the varsity backfield. It proved to Andy, though, that he had more speed than he had dared hope, and that he had cleared his first football hurdle. It was a consolation, too, to learn that Jerry Holt, the man who had led the pack, was a bright sprinting prospect for the Pelican track team.

Coach Todd gave the squad another tough calisthenic session, then sent them through another sprint in which Andy once more finished second to Jerry Holt. Andy could not be entirely sure, but he had the feeling that Todd was watching him with considerable interest. It gave him a quick boost until another old familiar feeling wormed its way in to smother the brief moment of elation. Todd was probably just treating himself to a better look at Jocko Baker's son.

There were more calisthenics and more running before Todd finally let the weary men plod in to take their showers. Andy tried his best to leave the field without revealing the depth of his fatigue. The others also probably tried, but there were several stumbles and near falls. Harry Todd had put them through the wringer.

It was a sample of the days to come. It was, admittedly, a crash program, designed to eliminate the unfit and to unearth whatever talent might be hidden in these men with little previous experience. Andy weathered it, sustained by doggedness and whatever else it takes to force a man beyond his limit. He gave his best to each assignment, trying to add a little extra to the effort. He moved in a fog of weariness for several days, and then his body became hardened to the punishment.

He admitted to himself how little he actually knew about the game of football. He was smart enough to reject whatever previous ideas he had formed that were cluttering up his mind. He was able, therefore, to absorb the things he learned, accepting them as entirely new ideas.

It was frightening how much there was to learn, a revelation which brought frequent stabs of doubt. Coach Todd, fighting against time, had no chance to drill his men on finer points of football. He was restricted to the simple fundamentals together with a lot of slam-bang body contact, but even these simple fundamentals opened a new and complicated world to Andy, scientific wonders such as balance, leverage, and proper timing.

His bright new uniform embarrassed him no longer, because it was no longer bright and new. The squad had been issued pads and helmets by this time, and a few sessions with the tackling dummy, plus some scrimmage work, had ground the dirt in nicely, permitting Andy to feel like one of the boys. It was a boost to his morale.

He got another boost during the early scrimmage periods. He settled a question that had bothered him. He could take it. He could soak up punishment, recover quickly, and come back for more, a vitally important factor distinguishing the rugged player from the one who is too easily injured. Great football talent, Andy knew, is worthless if the owner of the talent is the brittle type who watches too many games from the side line.

The daily scrimmage sessions taxed Coach Todd's ingenuity. Lacking enough men for two full teams was only part of it—he also lacked the proper balance between backfield men and linemen. It was necessary, therefore, to rotate the backfield candidates in the line. He showed no partiality. He also offered some sound logic to forestall objections from backfield men who might feel that line play was beneath them.

"Look at it this way," he suggested. "There will be plenty of times when a backfield man will find it important to know how a lineman thinks and how he is supposed to act, so if you get in there now and learn some of it firsthand it might come in mighty useful later on."

Andy, no different from other backfield men, could think of nothing less appealing than the workhorse job of tackle, guard, or center. He felt that, lacking the weight of a plunging fullback, or the necessary experience of a quarterback, what talent he possessed would be more effective in one of the halfback spots.

However, he was quick to understand the common sense behind Todd's words, so when a line assignment fell to him he gave it everything he had. He tried to act like a lineman and to think like a lineman, and once he forced himself into the mood he found the problems of a lineman much more complicated than he had suspected. He tried to solve them all as best he could, and, in the process, learned a lot of information that he tucked carefully aside for future use.

The scrimmage sessions, ragged as they were, were bone-jarring affairs. The men played as if someone stood behind them with a whip, which, in a sense, Coach Todd was doing. The whip was merely a notebook and a pencil, but it served the purpose. The notebook came out frequently and the pencil made notations. It reached the point where Todd's brief jottings drew some worried glances. Each man assumed that he might be the object of Todd's observations, but none knew just how bad, or good, the observation might turn out to be. As a consequence each man played a little harder.

It soon became obvious to Andy that Todd was not striving for perfection. The time was much too limited. Todd's objective seemed to be no more than a rough analysis of each man's football potential. He gave them simple problems, watching for alertness or confusion, weighing their strength against their brains, together with their willingness to work. He kept a close record of these things as tension mounted. He would hand down his decisions soon. Some of these men would no longer need their uniforms. The chosen few could look forward to another bitter fight ahead. Andy tried, without too much success, to keep his mind on other things.

One of the diversions Andy manufactured for himself was a return visit to the domain of Mike the pelican. He had permitted himself some amused speculation with regard to his first meeting with the grotesque bird. It is doubtful, though, that he would have tried to renew the acquaintance or to put his popularity to further test had it not been for his deliberate efforts to sidetrack his thoughts from the football situation.

On his next visit to Mike's stamping ground Andy was not foolhardy enough to take anything for granted. He had strong doubts about Mike's ability to remember anything from one fish to the next, so he approached the reunion with the caution it deserved. He remained upon the safety of the path.

Mike, dozing on the bank of his private lake, heard the sound of footsteps on the path. He shook himself awake and cocked a belligerent eye in Andy's direction. Mike took a double take, let out a croak which sounded friendly, then started with his awkward waddle toward the visitor.

There was no doubt, after that, that Mike's memory was good or that he recognized in Andy the same thing he had recognized before. He moved into the neutral territory of the path, edged up to Andy in an embarrassed sort of way, and lowered his head to be scratched. Andy obliged, feeling foolish even though he experienced an odd pleasure that the ill-tempered bird had accepted him as a pal. Andy made the scratching business as brief as possible, hoping no one was a witness to the scene. He left as soon as good manners would permit, but the moment, short as it was, had served its purpose, taking Andy's mind from football for a little while at least.

Sam Tedder was quick to recognize this need in

Andy. He spent a lot of time with Andy and was always welcome. Sam's calm acceptance of the things about him created a peaceful atmosphere. Sam, normally easygoing, enjoyed the added benefit of having his football worries virtually eliminated. His power at center had fulfilled Coach Hagerty's hopes, and Sam was now accepted as a first-string man.

Sam was good medicine for Andy. His mind was flexible and his opinions, for the most part, sound. Considerable of their conversation was devoted to skin diving, with Andy becoming more and more convinced that the big man knew the subject well.

Sam helped Andy over some rough spots, and Andy was grateful for the boost. He could not help but wonder, though, if he might need Sam's help a whole lot more when Coach Todd made his final choice of men who were varsity material.

The fateful day inevitably arrived. Todd made his announcement following the final workout. He called the squad about him with the reluctant air of a man not relishing the job ahead. He kept his eyes upon the notebook rather than upon the strained faces of the players. Andy felt a paralyzing pressure in his chest.

Todd cleared his throat before saying gruffly, "I'm sorry I don't have good news for all of you. I can only suggest that those of you I have been forced to drop will give it another try next year. You've got to understand that Judd Hagerty's requirements are pretty stiff. I can only recommend five men."

He started reading swiftly as if eager to finish the

unpleasant task. The name of Jerry Holt, the speedster, headed the list. Todd rattled off three other names. He hesitated briefly before saying, "Andy Baker."

Andy feared for several dizzy seconds that his legs would fold. His vision, momentarily blurred, seemed reluctant to return to normal. His breath, when he finally forced it from his lungs, rushed out with choking force. He was still in a mild daze when he received congratulations. There were a few, however, who did not congratulate him.

He heard a voice say bitterly, "I might have made the grade, too, if my old man had been a big wheel in this school."

The words sliced off a great big chunk of Andy's satisfaction. The same thought, he was sure, ultimately would have occurred to him, but it was rough to have it tossed in his teeth at a time like this.

Todd heard the crack and bristled to defend himself as well as Andy. The man who had sounded off, however, was already heading for the gym. Todd shrugged and let him go. He motioned to Andy who obeyed the gesture, relieved to find that his legs would carry him that far.

Todd said, "You made it on your own, Andy. Do you believe me?"

Andy hesitated briefly before saying, "Yes, I believe you."

Todd studied him carefully. "But you've still got your fingers crossed. Is that it?"

Andy forced a reluctant nod, hastening to explain,

"It's not that I doubt your judgment, Coach. It's just that—" His voice trailed off as he made a helpless gesture with his hands.

Todd said thoughtfully, "I know what's bugging you, of course. I know the spot you're in. The point is, Andy, you won't get very far in football if you let your mind stay cluttered up with doubts." He paused, then added shrewdly, "You'll never be entirely sure until you prove beyond question that you're varsity caliber."

"No," conceded Andy ruefully.

CHAPTER

5

In the days that followed Andy found but little time to clutter up his mind with doubts. He was much too busy, mentally and physically, with the exciting process of mastering a new science. Even though he was prepared for a vast difference between prep-school and college football, he was frankly amazed at the labyrinth of technicalities ahead of him.

He faced them eagerly, cramming his brain at the blackboard sessions, and trying to absorb the essential points in the football movies they were shown. All of this was strictly theory—the trick was to put the theory into practice on the football field. He tried, as all the rest were trying, not entirely sure of the progress he was making. He made mistakes, but so did other men. There were also brief, satisfying moments when everything clicked nicely.

The practice field was a daily mass of movement. The men were divided into squads to simplify the work of the coaching staff, but Judd Hagerty refused to designate the squads by name or number, letting each man believe he was a member of the varsity until the big day came when Hagerty would make his final choice of men whom he considered varsity material. Meanwhile he covered lots of ground with no apparent show of haste. No man could ever be quite sure that Hagerty was not watching him. Andy was pleased to learn that Harry Todd would coach the group of backfield men to which he had been assigned.

It was born in on Andy gradually that the Pelicans, even in these practice sessions, appeared to be showing an unnatural tension, a hard-eyed grimness dominating all their play. It was apparent even in the veterans who were assured of first-string positions on the team. These men were driving themselves as hard as those who were battling to keep from being dropped when Hagerty made his final cut. Andy mentioned it to Sam who, even in these early stages, had obviously nailed down his spot in the center of the line.

"I noticed it too," admitted Sam.

"Got any theories? You're closer to the first-string men than I am."

"Yes," Sam said thoughtfully, "I guess I have. Most of the men who have played under Hagerty think he's the best coach in the world. No one mentions it, but I'm sure they're still burned up over that effigy deal. They want to give Hagerty a winning season and rub it in the hair of those who think he should be bounced."

"That figures. What are the chances?"

They were sitting in Andy's room. Sam shifted his

big body, making the chair creak. "I think they're
pretty good," he said at last. "Every man who played for
us last year should be improved this year—a matter of
experience. We've got some real good sophomores with
a lot of talent. There's always a big *if,* though, connected with sophomores when they get their first chance
at big-time college play, because no matter how good
they finally might get to be, their lack of experience is
bound to be a handicap."

"*That* I can understand," said Andy grimly.

Sam summed it up with, "It's a tossup. Hagerty's got
the material if it clicks. The weak spot, this year, is
liable to be on the bench. He hasn't had a chance yet
to be sure of his reserves. Most of the guys know this,
and they're worried. They want to chalk up a big season for the old man."

"That answers my question," Andy said. "I only hope
I'll be in there to help them."

"And that goes double," Sam said earnestly. He
abruptly changed the subject. "When are we going to
get in a little scuba work?"

Andy shrugged, confessing, "I sure miss it. It's the
one thing I can count on to untie my nerves. Looks sort
of hopeless, though, with football every day."

"There's Sunday," Sam suggested.

"I've thought about it, naturally," said Andy. "The
trouble is I'm not in a position to risk anything the
coach might not approve of. If I barged right up and
asked him, he might say 'No,' and that would be the
end of it."

"You've got a point there," said Sam. "Well, maybe it'll work out somehow."

"I hope so. My brain's so full of things I'm trying to remember about football that I'm afraid some of it's liable to pop out through the top of my head. If I could loaf around under water for a while I might keep my skull from getting punctured."

Andy's need for a brief diversion from the churning thoughts of football was fulfilled the following day, though not in a way he would have chosen. His father made one of his occasional visits to his alma mater, arriving in his own four-motored plane, surrounded by his usual retinue of private secretaries and gag writers, together with a few companions capable of giving out convincing belly laughs when Jocko said something he considered funny and raised his eyebrows as a signal for appreciation.

Jocko had phoned Andy from New York that morning to announce his arrival late in the afternoon, and Andy had been guiltily relieved that football practice would prevent him from meeting his father at the airport.

"That's okay, son," Jocko's voice had boomed across the wire. "Just meet me at the cottage when you've washed the sweat off, and we'll go into St. Pete for a big feed."

Andy made several absent-minded blunders on the field that afternoon, annoyed with himself for permitting the visit of his father to throw him off the beam, particularly at this time when all of his concentration should be devoted to the game of football. At the end of the practice session he took his shower, then went to his room to change clothes for the meeting with his father.

The "cottage" was a twelve-room, Florida-style ranch house with an enclosed patio surrounding a small swimming pool. Jocko rented it by the year to accommodate him and his guests whenever he felt like flying down to see how things were getting on at good old Gulf. It was a short walk from the campus to the cottage.

Andy covered the distance slowly, still plagued by a feeling of annoyance. He was annoyed, primarily, at himself for his inability to adjust himself to his dad's profession, his way of living, and his personality. Andy blamed the failure on himself, clinging to the conviction that there had to be something admirable beneath Jocko's flashy surface, and that Andy, as a son, was duty bound to find it.

It might be quite a job, he reflected grimly, yet a job well worth the effort to establish a normal father and son relationship. Andy had a deep desire for this, and in fleeting moments of the past he was certain he had sensed the same urge in his dad. There was a gap to cross—a bridge to build.

Andy entered the cottage, crossed the spacious living room, and headed toward the noisy conversation on the patio. His father, facing the doorway, saw him first. He heaved his bulk from a deck chair with some difficulty.

"Andy, my boy!" he roared. "Come in, son! Come in! Glad to see you!"

Jocko was a large, big-barreled man, showing the sleekness of good living, Turkish baths, and strong masseurs. His round head, semi-bald, looked rounder than it usually did when topped by the toupee he always wore on stage. He gave Andy the big handshake, then, without turning, uttered a peremptory, "Shoo!"

The half-dozen other people on the patio were there, then they were not there. They disappeared like scuttling mice. It was, to Andy's thinking, a distasteful show of force, a reaction which showed briefly in his eyes before he could prevent it.

Jocko was quick to catch the implied criticism. His own eyes hardened with a quick anger which he mastered promptly. "I'm sorry, kid," he said gruffly. "But—well, that's the way things are in this rat race. The hired help expect it and get paid for it. But then, I guess you wouldn't understand."

"I guess not," Andy said, ashamed too late of his primly stuffy manner. Things were off to a bad start.

Jocko, as he always did, took prompt charge of the situation. His affability returned as if someone had touched a valve. "Sit down, kid! Sit down! You're lookin' great. I was sure proud to learn you'd made the varsity."

"Take it easy, Dad," Andy said with a grin, trying to get into the spirit of the thing. "I haven't made it yet. I'm still fighting for a spot."

Jocko waved all doubt aside with an expansive gesture. "You'll make it, kid, you'll make it. You're a chip off the old block."

Andy reserved comment on the statement, giving his father time to think it over. Andy then experienced one of those brief, swift moments when Jocko permitted him to guess at what might be going on beneath the flashy shell he had built about himself.

Jocko shrugged resignedly and said, "Nuts. Who am I trying to kid? I was a lead-footed bench warmer. I guess that's why I want to see a son of mine in the first-string Pelican line-up."

"I'll try to get there, Dad."

"Yes, sure," said Jocko with the half-scared look of a man who had almost permitted his emotions to get out of hand. He brought himself severely back in character. "How's the skin diving?"

"No time for it," Andy said regretfully. "Too much football."

"Well now," Jocko said aggressively. "I can handle *that* all right. I'll have a little talk with Hagerty."

"Please don't," said Andy flatly.

"Why not?" demanded Jocko, bristling. "I still have a *little* pull around this school, and that half-baked coach won't be around long anyway."

"Who says so?" Andy asked, still in the same flat tone.

Jocko took a good look at his son; then his eyes widened at what he saw. He controlled his rising anger for the second time. "I'm sorry, kid," he said, "but I can't very well let go once I've got my teeth set in a thing."

Andy knew the futility of combating such a statement. He compromised by saying, "He deserves another chance this year."

"He'll get it."

There was an uncomfortable, short silence. Andy steadied himself with a deep breath before tackling a tricky subject. "You may think I'm trying to buck you just for kicks. I've got a better reason. You're a big wheel in this school, Dad—but I don't have to tell you that. The point is, it puts me in a mighty uncomfortable position. The only distinction I have around the place is the fact that I'm your son. It makes me quite a prominent figure, I'll admit, but it's not the sort of prominence I've earned myself. In other words, I'd like to accomplish something on my own without any outside help."

Another silence. Having summoned courage to declare himself, Andy had no way of knowing how the declaration might be met. His best guess was that Jocko would resent it and would move in promptly to defend himself. It appeared, for a moment, that Andy had guessed right. Jocko swelled up momentarily, then deflated. He scrubbed a big hand across his mouth.

"Yes," he said. Then another thoughtful, "Yes. Too bad you had to spell it out for me, but honest, kid, I'm not as stupid as I sometimes try to act. Throwing my weight around and pulling strings has got to be a habit with me. I see your point, and I agree with it." He grinned, a rare sort of grin for Jocko—nothing phony about it this time. "I won't try to meddle any longer with the things you want to do, and I hope I'm not too late in wiseing up."

Andy covered his surprised relief as best he could. He was trying to form the proper words of thanks when Jocko reverted quickly to the professional comedian. "Let's eat," he suggested heartily. "I'm hungry enough to chase a kangaroo."

Jocko had reserved a table at a large, expensive restaurant. He entered in the bouncing manner of a man expecting to be recognized. He was. The dinner chatter stopped, to be replaced by excited muttering as heads were turned to follow Jocko's progress toward his table. Andy felt like a pet being led on a leash.

Once seated, Jocko said, "That's the way it is, kid, and you've got to learn to live with it." Then, in a burst of frankness, he added, "Luckily, I like it."

It came as no surprise to Andy when the dinner turned out to be something of an ordeal. There was no lack of conversation, because Jocko was accomplished in this field, and Andy managed to uphold his end. The strain was there, however, the underlying tension of two people wanting earnestly to find a common meeting ground, of a father and son placed in the ridiculous position of being virtually strangers with no way to establish further closeness. Andy was glad when the evening finally ended, and was ashamed of himself for being glad.

Jocko Baker showed up at the football field next day to watch the practice. He came either through an honest urge to see his son in action, or because he felt impelled to prove that he was welcome anywhere at Gulf. Whatever his motive, he soon learned he was not popular with the Pelicans. Judd Hagerty ignored him, and the players scowled when they glanced in his direction. Jocko stuck it out, however, his face set in stubborn lines.

It was a bad afternoon for Andy, made even worse because he could not pinpoint what was wrong with him. He only knew that he was playing football like a duffer, drawing mental blanks when his mind should have been upon the game, and missing tackles which he should have made.

He could not decide what caused it. He partially accepted the theory that he was trying too hard to impress his dad, that a quality of desperation sneaked into his added efforts, thereby fouling his co-ordination. On the other hand, he might have been trying too hard to impress the Pelicans, instinctively trying to prove that at least one member of the Baker family had the welfare of the Pelicans at heart. The sticky problem remained unsolved, and Andy hoped devoutly that his football lapse was temporary.

CHAPTER

6

WHEN Jocko Baker returned to the job of entertaining the nation, Andy's football game came back to normal. He accepted the matter gratefully, refusing to delve further into the why's and wherefore's of his brief slump. He had something else to think about—the rapidly approaching day when the Pelican squad would be reduced in size, when the ax would fall on those who had failed to make the grade.

Judd Hagerty went through the process of elimination as fairly as he could. He staged a short series of full-length games, permitting the men to play under the same conditions they might expect to find in actual competition. There would be a full complement of officials who would conduct the game according to the rules. Each team would have its coach with complete authority to run the team as he saw fit.

Hagerty, with a pair of his most reliable staff members, would sit in judgment, watching for brilliance, mediocrity, and flaws. They already possessed exacting charts on each man who had not, as yet, proved himself to be varsity material. The charts told many things which would have surprised the man himself. What the charts did not tell was how these men might act in the heat of competition, how they would stand up under pressure.

And the pressure would be on. Hagerty would see to it. He let it be clearly understood that these elimination games would be for keeps, that the men on the doubtful list were receiving their final chance, and that their showing in these games would determine their football future with the Pelicans. It was a bowl game for the doubtfuls, one of the most important they would ever play. The games would be held in the formidable stadium, and the public was invited to attend.

When the day for Andy's final tryout pulled around he was feeling awful—exactly the way Hagerty had intended him and others like him to feel—hollow on the inside, feverish on the outside, racked with doubts and trembling with determination. If a man could take this combination of emotions into a game and still play creditable football, Hagerty could be assured the man was worth attention.

Andy tried to assay, as reasonably as possible, the qualities he had to offer and the things he might depend on. For the most part, it was encouraging. There was no further trace of his prep-school awkwardness. He had speed and a pair of big, sure hands which seemed to fit the football. He could handle a bullet forward pass with considerable assurance, and his footwork in an open field was tricky, with the promise of improvement. He had learned to memorize and translate signals with speed and accuracy.

On the debit side was inexperience, a fact he must accept, no matter how reluctantly. There had been times in practice scrimmage when his reaction to a situation was slow. A veteran, having been in the same spot many times before, would have reacted automatically, through habit. Andy, on the other hand, had to reach into his mental file system for an answer to the thing he had been taught. It took time, not much time of course, but a fraction of a second can mean the difference between a first down and a loss. Andy tried to force his mind from such uncertainties.

The teams, designated as the Blues and the Greens, had been selected a few days in advance, allowing the coaches only a short time to drill the squads. This, too, was a calculated part of Hagerty's system. It gave him an insight into each man's alertness and adaptability by proving how readily a man could master a new set of plays and signals, even though the new plays had to be reasonably simple. Time was too limited to teach more complicated stuff.

Andy was glad to learn that Harry Todd would coach the Blue team, to which Andy had been assigned. The squads had been balanced as carefully as possible in order that neither team would have too much of an advantage. Varsity men had been moved in to maintain the balance. The exception was at quarterback. Hagerty assigned none of his regulars to this spot, hoping to unearth some new talent for the exacting job of running a team. Jerry Holt would quarterback the Blues, and Sam Tedder would be in the center of the line.

When the big day finally came, Andy was more than willing to lean against Sam's calm assurance. Even so, Andy's nerves were in bad shape before game time. His attack of nerves was heightened when he learned that Mark Sutton would play halfback on the opposing Greens.

Andy, to this point, had avoided contact with Mark Sutton, a matter which had required small effort on his part during the frantic rush of early training. Mark, like Andy, had been too busy with other things to let personalities intrude. The truce had been made easier by the fact that the two men trained in different groups. Contact would be made today, however—plenty of it. Andy, in a way, felt a tingle of anticipation. On the other hand, he resented a setup which might give Mark a chance to sidetrack Andy's concentration on the job at hand. On this day in particular he wanted to play the best football at his command.

When he entered the big bowl of the stadium for the warm-up session, Andy found that a large portion of the student body, as well as a sizable crowd of outsiders, had accepted the invitation for free entertainment. They had learned, from past experience, that these final tryout games staged by Hagerty could be slam-bang affairs with so many players on the field fighting desperately for a permanent spot with the

Pelicans. The fans might not see football at its best, but they would see plenty of ferocious action.

Todd had placed Andy in the starting line-up at right half. Andy was grateful for the honor, even though he was not entirely sure he wanted the extra load of this responsibility. He was not gaining what he had hoped to gain from the warm-up, the feeling of assurance that ten other men would be with him on the team to do their share. The football did not feel as he wanted it to feel, buoyant and full of life. It seemed a little heavy, unwilling to stay safely in his hands. He traced the trouble to his fingers. They were stiff and not entirely steady.

The Blues won the toss, electing to receive. Andy's speed drew him a downfield position near the goal line, one of the spots at which a good kickoff was most likely to arrive. Jerry Holt was in the center spot, flanked on the other side by the fullback, Ralph Hopper, a first-string varsity man. Andy's throat was dry and his knees were weak as he watched the kicker tee the ball on the Green forty-yard line. Andy hoped, with only a small sense of guilt, that the ball would not be kicked to him.

His hope was realized. It was a fine boot right down the center of the field. Holt scarcely had to move from where he stood on the five-yard line. He displayed a rush of nerves by jigging around uncertainly. Andy almost forgot his own nerves in the fear that Holt might miss the catch. Holt managed to get under it, however. He bobbled it a little, but once he had it safely in his hands his confidence returned along with his sound football instincts. Instead of uncorking his full sprinting speed, he held back for his interference.

This was Andy's job, and he went about it a fraction of a second later than was necessary, stumbling slightly as he tried to get his legs in motion. Once assured that they would bear his weight, he felt the strength flow back into them. He picked the biggest man within his range, unaware that he was about to attempt a key block which, if successful, might shake Holt loose for yardage. Andy hurled himself into the block with more enthusiasm than common sense. He committed himself too soon, starting his lunge a full stride sooner than he should have started it, thereby giving the intended victim ample warning. The big man swerved, giving Andy a large chunk of open air through which to sail. The flight was brief. Andy landed in a disjointed sort of way, feeling like a fool. The man whom he had missed drove through to drop Holt on the sixteen-yard line.

Andy, at the moment, would have traded places with a mole, so that he could dig a hole in the ground and quickly disappear in it. Having no such talent, Andy forced himself to stand erect with the idea of apologizing to Holt and to his teammates, an intention which was sidetracked by Mark Sutton. He moved close to Andy, a mocking grin behind his face guard.

"That was a terrific block you just threw, Andy," complimented Mark. "It showed real class. You're just the sort of man Judd Hagerty's looking for."

Andy felt a flare of anger, but was too disgusted with himself to let the anger have its way. He turned away from Mark and went up to Holt. "Sorry, Jerry," he said briefly. "I goofed on that one."

"Forget it. I almost fouled up the catch. That tackle helped my nerves, though. Do you feel better too?"

"Yes," Andy said mechanically. Then, as he headed toward the huddle, he learned with considerable surprise that he *did* feel better despite the clumsy exhibition he had just pulled off. The brief action had dispelled his fog, and his hand, as he held it out in front of him, was steady. He tested his lungs. They, too, had loosened up, so that he could breathe deeply.

Holt sensibly called a line play on the first down. The Blues were too deep in their own territory to try anything fancy at this stage. They needed running room. An open play would also require more delicate timing, and Holt probably reasoned it was wise to give the relatively untried men a chance to settle down before subjecting them to something complicated. He also called Ralph Hopper's number on the first play, another smart precaution, because Hopper, a veteran, was less likely to mess things up in the early stages of the game. Jerry, furthermore, tried to use his head by sending Hopper through the Greens' left guard, one of the inexperienced hopefuls aiming at the varsity.

The play was well conceived, the strategy was sound. There was only one thing wrong with it. It failed to work. The Green left guard was primed with all the desperation of a man who had to prove himself, and who had waited a long time for this moment. His reaction was clumsy but effective, backed by the explosive, unexpected strength of a fanatic. He met the charge with a huge grunt, wrapping himself around Ralph Hopper like an octopus, and hauled him down at the line of scrimmage.

Returning to the huddle, Hopper asked bewilderedly, "Where did he *get* all those arms and legs?" No one could enlighten him.

Holt, hiding his disappointment, decided to abandon caution. He called a signal for a play that required a bit of ball handling behind the line, a play designed to use Holt's speed. He took the ball from Sam, performed a quarter spin, and faked a belly hand-off to Ralph Hopper. Hopper blasted to his right off-tackle, hoping to draw the Green defense in that direction. The deception was good and reasonably effective, because the Greens were obviously expecting Hopper to carry a large part of the offensive load.

Holt, meanwhile, hid the ball behind his hip while the rest of the Blue backfield, after a deliberate hesitation, headed fast toward the left to form a wall of interference for Holt. The Blue right guard came from the line to cut across and join the interference.

Andy's blocking assignment on the play was flexible, depending on how far the Green line-backers had been drawn out of position by Hopper's line buck. If they recovered quickly, Andy was to nail the man who posed the greatest threat to Holt. It was a decision he would have to make.

The play began to look as if it might succeed. The other Blue halfback, Ned Carter, had drawn the definite assignment of putting the Green right end out of business, a job which he accomplished neatly. The left side of the Blue line was holding solidly, allowing the wide end sweep to maintain its pattern.

The need to atone for his first blunder piled a little extra pressure upon Andy. He tried to make allowance for this pressure, to remain alert, and to pick his target wisely. Then suddenly there were a lot of targets as the Green line-backers recognized the line plunge as a fake. Andy tried to pick the one who looked most dangerous. He threw his block, knowing instantly that overeagerness had fouled him up again. He threw the block too soon.

He got a break, however, a break completely undeserved. Mark Sutton handed it to him, presenting the gift through overeagerness as strong as Andy's. Mark, obviously, had wanted the pleasure of bashing into Andy, and in order to attain it he had collided with his own teammate. The result was in Andy's favor. Mark's blunder made the sloppy block look beautiful. Both men were now in line with it, and before they could get out of line the pair of them were sprawled upon the turf. Holt cut through the hole and peeled off eighteen yards before they ran him out of bounds.

When Mark got off the ground he had no wisecracks up his sleeve. He had messed the play up, and he knew it. His worried glance toward the side line proved his guilt. He was hoping Hagerty had not seen his blunder, a feeble hope at best. Andy, too, was guilty of the hope he might get credit for a spectacular block, another feeble hope which he discarded promptly. He had been lucky, and, as he well knew, a football player cannot depend on luck.

The Blues, particularly the doubtfuls, the men with so much at stake, were nicely steamed up over their long first down. Andy absorbed some of the excitement in the huddle, an excitement that almost choked him when he heard his signal called. Cold sweat spurted in his palms. He wiped them furtively against his pants. Jerry Holt had called a draw play, a gambling sort of play depending entirely on whether or not the opposing lineman permits himself to be mousetrapped. In the event the victim solves the play in time, refusing to accept the bait, small blame can be placed on the ball carrier if he fails to gain. The play depended largely upon luck, which meant that Andy could not be held responsible for bad luck.

Holt had chosen his intended sucker wisely—the same left guard who had stopped the opening play from scrimmage, and who, it was hoped, would still be trembling for the chance to sacrifice life and limb for the dear old Greens. If his high ambition still held strong, the play might well succeed.

It got off to a good start. The guard co-operated with everything he had, ignoring all previous warning about mousetraps. He came charging like a wild-eyed buffalo through the opening which had thoughtfully been left for him. He came barreling into the Blue backfield where he was decked by a solid block from Hopper.

Andy, after the short count, took an accurate belly pass from Holt and headed toward the hole with all the speed he had, whipped by the frantic urge to demonstrate his real ability. His momentum was great enough to shake off the clawing hand of a Green lineman. He blasted into the Green backfield, running with more power than cunning. They hauled him down after a four-yard gain.

Four yards, of course, was nothing to be taken lightly, except that Andy knew, beyond the shadow of a doubt, that the yardage should have been considerably more. The pattern of the play was as clear as a blueprint in his mind. He could recall the exact position of each Green line-backer, and, just as clearly, he could see now what he should have done to cross them up. He had to assume, therefore, that this same knowledge was available to him the instant he crossed the line of scrimmage, that he had known exactly what to do, yet, under the whip of urgency, had been unable to co-ordinate his feet and brain.

How long would this condition handicap him? The thought scared him. He could tell himself, of course, "Now just relax. This is just another football game." But this was *not* just another football game. It was a game which could quite easily be the turning point in Andy Baker's life.

CHAPTER

7

ANDY kept his fears from getting out of hand by centering his hopes upon the fact that the game was still in its early stages. He kept repeating to himself that the high-speed action still ahead would shake his nerves back into their proper slots. When this condition came about, he could concentrate on football rather than upon this game's significance and how it might affect his future. The big catch was—how long would it take for him to find out whether this was so?

It did not take long. The Blues had the ball on their thirty-eight-yard line, second down, six yards to go. Holt called another wide one, giving himself the carrying assignment. It was an option play which had a chance to work because Holt, in practice, had developed a fine passing arm together with an accuracy which promised to improve with experience. The Greens had undoubtedly been warned that Holt's passing game might prove a threat. On this play Holt would shoot at his target if he had one open. If the eligible receivers were covered, it would probably mean that the Green defense would be loosened up enough for Holt to attempt a run. The choice was up to him.

The opening action would take place on the right side of the Blue line. The right end would stay put to protect Holt if he decided to run. The left end would cut in toward the center of the field, and Andy, the other possible receiver, would stay close to the left side line. The play got under way smoothly. Holt faded, his arm cocked, looking for a receiver in the open. The Blue forward wall held stubbornly to give Holt good protection.

This much of the play registered on Andy before he went about his own business, the assignment of reaching the side line at a spot ten yards beyond the line of scrimmage. At this point he would turn and look for the pass, and, as he ran, he was hoping in a guilty sort of way that the pass would not come at him.

It was wasted apprehension. Something else came at him instead—Mark Sutton, moving with all the driving force his legs could generate. In the brief flash of remaining time before he was hit, Andy realized Mark was taking a long chance with this sort of pass defense while still uncertain that a pass was in the making. If a pass was already on its way toward Andy, interference would be called. Mark, furthermore, was eliminating himself from the play without knowing if he might be needed elsewhere. Andy's split-second decision, for what it might be worth, told him that Mark's football strategy was questionable.

There was nothing questionable about the block. Andy tried a belated swerve which unbalanced him enough to make him more vulnerable. Mark hit him from the side, driving a shoulder savagely against Andy's ribs. Andy landed on his back with Mark on top of him. Mark, making a hasty show of getting up to join the play, managed to grind an elbow into Andy's exposed throat.

Andy had doubted, for a moment, that he could get off the ground. This, however, was before the elbow episode. The muscles of his body exploded with his temper. Black anger yanked him to his feet. His voice came out in a hoarse croak. "You no-good slob!"

He was speaking to Mark's back. Mark was hurrying dutifully, though much too late, toward the scene of action, a pile-up on the forty-two-yard line. Holt obviously had failed to find a receiver open, and had carried the ball himself.

None of which concerned Andy at the moment. Driven by a rage which words would never satisfy, he was gaining fast on Mark when he bumped into something solid and unmoving. He tried a detour, but Sam Tedder held him back with a big hand on each arm.

"Let me go!" snarled Andy.

"No dice," refused Sam calmly. "Take it easy."

When Andy refused to follow his advice, Sam gave him a quick shake. Andy's head bobbled on his shoulders, but the treatment jarred some of his senses back in place, making him more receptive to Sam's next words.

"For Pete's sake, Andy, use your brain a little. If you start a brawl with Sutton, you'll get booted from the game. Is that what you want?"

Sam made his point. Andy swallowed a lump of apprehension as he realized how close he had come to doing what Mark had wanted him to do—start a fight. Mark had played him for a sucker, and Andy had responded like a sucker. The dangerous flame of Andy's anger cooled a bit, but the smoldering embers were still active.

Jerry Holt was now faced with a third down, two yards to go. He had a seasoned power runner in Ralph Hopper, a bull of a man who would have a first-rate chance of blasting out a first down through the line, but Holt showed his true potential as a quarterback who has to gamble now and then when the odds are right. He must have reasoned that the Green team would be virtually certain he would call on Hopper. It made sense all the way. Instead, his signal called for Hopper to fake a plunge into the line. The rest of the signal called for a swift strike at the other side of the line with Andy carrying the ball. If the line-backers could be pulled across to cover Hopper, the play would hinge on Andy's ability to get past the line of scrimmage into a disorganized Green backfield.

When Andy heard his signal, he expected his stomach to do a flip-flop as it had before when the assignment came to him. He was surprised when his innards stayed in place. He was further surprised at a quick tingle of anticipation which seemed out of place, a feeling he did not attempt to analyze. It was there, and that was that. It felt good, too.

The play broke well. Holt's ball handling was smooth. He faked a belly hand-off to the charging Hopper, completed his turn, and flipped an accurate shovel pass to Andy, who was heading toward the inside tackle spot. It looked for an instant as if his straining lineman might not make a hole for him, then Andy saw it open with the deliberation of slow motion on a movie film.

On any previous play Andy's frantic urgency would have sent him barreling into the backs of his own linemen. Something happened now, however, something over which he had no control. It was as if a forgotten, unused timing device began to function of its own accord. Andy checked his drive for a fraction of a second, long enough to let the hole get just a little wider.

It was still a puny opening, but Andy hit it hard, gaining speed. He felt the slap of reaching hands against his pants, a threat he shook off without breaking stride. Once in the Green backfield, Andy's timing gadget kept on working. He moved with smooth precision as opposed to the previous stampede he had attempted through the Green defenders.

The results were promptly evident, even though the line-backers had not been fooled as badly as they might have been. One of the halfbacks had been pulled into the trap, but there were still four more line-backers to contend with, inasmuch as the Greens had been using a six-man line.

Andy, cutting to the left, saw the deep man coming in at him, a strong threat to nail him before he could get far along the side line. A quick glance showed Mark Sutton, under a full head of steam, charging at him from the right. The computer in Andy's brain kept working at high speed, its message clear enough to control a strong temptation to crash into Mark head-on with driving knees. The moment introduced a greater challenge, offering Andy the chance to test his football skill. The computer told him that Mark's head of steam was greater than it should have been, that Mark's urge to get his hands on Andy was messing up his football brains.

The rest was reasonably simple, because Mark made it easy. His reckless tackle was premature, a matter Andy took advantage of by a slight swerve and a slight checking of his stride, a maneuver which placed Mark in a vulnerable position, spread out full length in the air. The palm of Andy's hand flashed out to smack a bull's-eye on Mark's helmet, thrusting downward at the same time to plow Mark's face into the turf. Andy used the force of the stiff arm to swing his own legs clear of Mark's clawing hands.

The meeting with Mark, though brief and satisfactory, slowed Andy down a bit, and gave the Green defenders a chance to get back in the game. Andy regained his stride in time to swivel off another five yards before they hauled him down. The total gain was thirteen yards, giving the Blues a first down in enemy territory on the forty-five-yard line.

Andy's teammates let him know how much they liked his run, but Andy scarcely heard the words or felt the slaps upon his back. His thoughts were fumbling with a mystery. What had happened to him in that short space of time? He had a couple of minutes to think it over when the Green captain called time out.

The matter was tied up in some way with Mark Sutton. Mark had caused Andy to blow his top. Andy could only conclude, therefore, that the surge of anger had steered his thinking along another route, that the rage had acted as a sedative to relieve the tension which this game had built up in him.

During the last play he had not tried to look impressive. He had forgotten, momentarily, that he was fighting for his football future, and that every move he made was being watched and catalogued. He had not attempted to drag past instructions from his brain and put them into use, he had merely let them pop out of their own accord, unhandicapped by fear and worry. It was a vast relief for him to learn that this could happen, that the football knowledge he had crammed into his mind was ready to flow out, so long as it was not impeded by a barrier of tension.

So much for theory. He forced himself to remember he had shown good stuff in the previous play, but that there were other plays to come, and the question still remained as to whether or not this first burst of talent would repeat itself. Andy took the only precaution he could think of. He concentrated on Mark Sutton, disliking the man as thoroughly as he could, an easy task.

He even allowed himself a small flash of amusement at the strange twist the game had taken. Before its start he had been afraid Mark's presence might distract him from the job at hand, and now he was depending on Mark's presence to keep his football at its peak.

Jerry Holt, quick to sense the change in Andy, made prompt use of his new offensive weapon. He gave Andy the ball-toting assignment on an end sweep. The play got off to a bad start. A Green lineman bulled through to mess it up, causing Andy to lose a couple of precious seconds while dodging him in his own backfield. As a consequence, the timing of the whole play was fouled up. Andy managed, though, to get back to the line of scrimmage before being piled up, which was quite a feat.

Despite the fact that the play went for no gain, Andy was not depressed by the result. He had kept his head and had swiftly analyzed the play. He was satisfied with his performance, which, he knew, could have been a lot worse.

Holt went to the air on the second down. Andy hurried down the side line to spot himself as an alternate receiver, but, in this instance, was not needed. The right end performed a deceptive buttonhook and was wide open for Holt's pass. The play went for twelve yards, bringing the ball to the Green thirty-three-yard line.

Holt called an option play. He faded for a pass, making it look convincing enough to scatter the Green defense. Seeing that the Green left end had been neatly blocked from the play, Holt tucked the ball beneath his arm and set out for pay dirt, with Andy sprinting out ahead of him.

The Green defenders came in fast. Andy tuned his brain to the pattern of the play, controlling his speed to an effective pace that would not throw him off balance when he had to throw a block. He had an early chance. A Green halfback was cutting across fast. Slightly behind him and closer to the goal line Mark Sutton was coming in for the kill. Andy, spotting both of them, was never quite sure whether football instinct or pure animosity governed his next move. At any rate, his swift decision told him that the first man would be a fraction of a second late to make a tackle, and that Mark Sutton posed the greater threat.

Andy, therefore, chose Mark as his target. He stifled the impulse to make prompt, violent contact, giving heed to the warning that a hasty block could easily make him look bad and Mark look good. So Andy timed it. He anticipated Mark's fake swerve and refused to fall for it. Instead, he struck with all the savagery he had while Mark was still off balance from the swerve.

His shoulder caught Mark just above the belt. When they hit the ground Mark served as Andy's mattress. Andy was in good shape when he reached his feet. Mark was in no hurry to get up. He was speechless, and his eyes, though slightly glassy, were filled with venom. Andy shot him a tight grin and walked away, elated to learn he had thrown the key block that had sprung

Holt loose for the first touchdown of the game. Holt kicked the extra point to make the score 7-0.

The Greens came fighting back. Andy, getting his first chance on defense, learned, with cautious satisfaction, that his reflexes were still working well, and that his football instincts were still sound, unsmothered by the rush of nerves which had handicapped him at the start. He had an early opportunity to keep his new line of thinking in the groove. He was given a chance to tackle Mark Sutton in the open. Andy smeared him with a tackle hard enough to cause a fumble. Unfortunately, the bobble was recovered by the Greens.

The tackle provided another boost to Andy's confidence. It also seemed to have its effect on the other members of the team. Their glances toward Andy seemed to say they had found a guy they could depend on. The Blue defense became noticeably stiffer. It finally stopped the Green drive on the Blue thirty-six-yard line. An out-of-bounds kick brought the ball in play on the seventeen-yard line.

The Blues got under way again, grinding out a pair of first downs before they stalled. There were a few fireworks but no serious threats during the remainder of the first period. The teams had been wisely chosen with regard to balance. Andy kept his own game in high gear by keeping Mark Sutton well in mind.

CHAPTER

8

Andy's concentration on Mark Sutton did not, apparently, affect his ability to think about football. An odd pattern of the play began to force its way into his thinking. Not until he had given it more study and was reasonably sure of his deductions did he mention it to Holt. He walked beside the quarterback when the teams changed goals to start the second period.

"Look, Jerry," Andy said, "I may be climbing the wrong tree, but I think I've stumbled on something you ought to know. It might pay off."

"Shoot," invited Holt.

"I don't think the varsity boys on the other team, or on our team either, are working up too big a sweat. They know they've got it made no matter what happens, so this game is just another workout so far as they're concerned."

Holt nodded, his interest rising.

"On the other hand," continued Andy, "the guys like us are really batting their brains out. They're making up in fight what they lack in experience. They can be dangerous, and it seems to me they're the strong points on the teams."

"I hadn't noticed," confessed Holt. "But you could be right. I'll admit I've been trying to steer most of my plays away from the varsity big shots. I take it you're suggesting I start aiming at them."

"It's worth a try," said Andy.

"Okay!"

When the Blues next had the ball, Holt went about the testing of Andy's theory. Before putting the idea into the works, however, he called time out and drew the men into a conference. "I may be shooting off my big mouth out of turn," he said. "But so long as I'm supposed to be running the team I might as well have my say. I think the varsity men on both teams are loafing, because they have nothing to prove. Let's try playing them for the soft spots and see what happens."

There were a few indignant snorts from the varsity men on the Blue squad. Ralph Hopper, the first of the regulars to speak up, proved he was a good football man. "Jerry's right," he declared flatly. "I, for one, haven't been putting out any more than I had to, and that probably holds true for the rest of you who don't have to worry about turning in your uniform. If we feel that way, the boys across the line are probably feeling that way too. I vote with Jerry. Let's zero in on them and see what happens."

The program was successful, not in an explosive way, but gradually and effectively. The Blue varsity men

seemed to enjoy the sneaky trick they were playing on
their teammates. Their own play became sharper and
more jolting while their Green victims gave ground
grudgingly, not quite sure, as yet, just what was happening to them. The Blues scored another touchdown
and a one-point conversion before the half had ended.

During the rest period Andy was sitting on a bench
near Jerry Holt when Todd came over to them looking pleased. He said, "You did a real smart job out
there, Jerry, by pegging the varsity men as weak spots.
Don't think I missed what was going on."

Holt flushed and swallowed hard. "It wasn't my
idea," he blurted. "It was Andy's. I intended to tell
you, Coach, but I didn't want to admit it out there on
the field. I figured that if the men believed I'd thought
it up they'd have more confidence in me."

Todd appraised Andy carefully, then nodded.
"You're both to be congratulated. You used your head,
Andy, and that's what you're out there for. You also
used yours, Jerry. A smart quarterback should accept
suggestions if he thinks they're any good. Furthermore,
it didn't do you any harm, Jerry, to tell me who came
up with the idea." He grinned and added, "It was a
fine idea while it lasted, but I think it's run its race.
I'll lay a bet against big odds that the Green varsity
boys are getting their ears chewed off about this time.
They won't be patsies in the second half."

Coach Todd was very right indeed. Having learned
they had been played for suckers, the varsity men on
the Green squad came out to avenge their honor in the

second half. The Blues were also well steamed up. With a nice lead to protect they settled grimly to the job.

Andy found himself in the middle of some high-speed action—plenty of it. He was satisfied, for the most part, with his game. It was not spectacular, but it was steady, a situation with which he had to be content. He was gaining in experience and was storing the information carefully away. He was encouraged by the fact that Todd had left him in the game, despite various replacements in other spots. He assumed Todd had a purpose.

He noticed that Mark Sutton was playing better football, suggesting that the Green coach had jumped on Mark with both feet during the half-time period. Mark had heeded the warning and was trying to co-ordinate his efforts with those of the other men.

Andy and Mark came into contact now and then, but the contact, though violent, was of a businesslike rather than personal nature. These meetings, nevertheless, continued to serve the vital purpose of supplying Andy with the stimulus to keep his mind from more distracting things. The change occurred halfway through the third period. Another halfback replaced Mark.

The significance of the move did not reach Andy right away. It acted in the nature of a delayed fuse—a sort of double take. He was concentrating hard on the next play when the substitution was made, and not until the play actually got under way did Andy tumble to the fact that Mark was missing from the Green backfield. Andy had a blocking assignment on that play, and, at such times, had schooled himself to keep an eye on Mark. When Mark failed to appear in the picture, Andy missed a block he should have made.

The shock began to spread through Andy, although he checked it angrily, slamming the lid on an apprehension which he knew was stupid and unreasonable. Why, he demanded of himself, should the absence of a single man from the opposing team affect his own brand of football? The answer was easy. It should not affect his game at all.

The answer, unfortunately, did not coincide with fact. Andy's brand of football for the next few plays was somewhat on the absent-minded side as he frantically tried to adjust himself to a new condition. He had not realized, until now, how much he had depended on Mark's goading influence, and now that the influence was no longer there he had to scramble for a substitute.

It helped a little to remember that he had been playing good sound football. Okay, he assured himself, he would continue to play good sound football. The assurance almost worked. Momentum carried him for several plays before it gradually began to dwindle, leaving Andy nothing to fall back on but the frightened knowledge that his football future was at stake, the familiar, urgent feeling he had brought with him into the game. He dared not falter at this stage. He dared not allow himself to believe that he required the sort of artificial stimulus Mark Sutton had provided.

Andy had no way of knowing what might have happened to him during the remainder of the game. Coach

Todd replaced him in the early minutes of the final period. Andy headed toward the bench, battling dismal thoughts. He had to assume he had been yanked from the line-up because he was no longer helping the Blue team. He clung, however, to the slender hope that Todd merely wanted to get a line on another backfield man, or that Todd might believe that Andy's ineffectiveness was caused by weariness. Todd gave no indication of what he might be thinking. He kept his attention on the game, while Andy took his place on the bench and tried to keep the strain from showing in his face. He kept his eyes upon the field without seeing what was going on. What difference did it make? Andy Baker had had his chance. The final selections would be posted on the following day. They would be ready when the men came in to dress for practice. Some of them would not have to dress.

Andy spent a restless night, waking frequently, his muscles cramped, his body damp with perspiration. He attended classes the next day, and gathered a few flunking grades when his mind refused to fasten on the subject. When he started for the gym that afternoon, he charted his course through the enclosed park at the Athletic Center, and the impulse to do so made him feel a little foolish. He was looking for a friendly gesture which he might cling to as an omen. Mike the pelican did not let him down. He waddled up to have his head scratched.

An anxious group of football players, not dressed for practice, were gathered in front of the bulletin board in the locker room. Their waiting tenseness informed Andy that the list had not as yet been posted. Andy added his own tenseness to the group. A quiver traveled through them when Coach Hagerty came into the room carrying a white sheet of paper in his hand. A path was quickly opened as he strode in toward the board. He jammed the paper in place with a pair of thumbtacks.

"I'm sorry it can't be all of you," he told them briefly.

He started from the room while the men surged toward the board. Andy was not fast enough to be among the leaders. He stood sweating on the outskirts. The first news of his fate came from one of the men inside the circle. A loud voice, harsh with disappointment, boomed out some familiar words.

"I wish *my* dad was a big shot in this school!"

Andy's stomach bucked as he interpreted the words, unpleasant as they were in one respect. He had made the varsity! He was afraid, for a moment, that the overpowering surge of vast relief might make him sick, but a quick diversion checked that possibility.

A voice, crackling with anger, barked, "Who said that?"

Hagerty had overheard the comment. He was striding once more toward the group, his jaw thrust out. He stopped and waited. The coach looked dangerous, formidable enough to freeze the tongues of those who faced him, and it was soon obvious that the guilty party had clammed up for keeps. There were, of course, no stool pigeons, so, after a reasonable wait, Hagerty let out a contemptuous snort and left the silent group.

When he was safely out of earshot the newly elected Pelicans congratulated one another in excited voices. The unlucky ones went moodily away. Once assured there would be no further mention of his own good fortune, Andy went to the board to confirm it. His name was there all right. For better or for worse, he was a varsity man.

His legs, still undependable from exultation and relief, managed to get him as far as his locker. He was still there, sitting on the bench and staring blankly at the steel door of his locker when Sam Tedder found him.

Sam said, "I told you so."

Andy nodded, then admitted, "I was scared."

"You can relax now, kid, you're in. I made the first string the easy way. You're doing it the hard way."

"I'm not there yet."

"The season's young." Then, trying to sound casual, "I met Hagerty outside. He wants to see you in his office right away."

"Huh?" demanded Andy, his nerves taking a violent jump. "What for?"

"Now cut it out!" said Sam sharply. "I don't know what he wants you for, but I know he's not going to slice you into little pieces."

Andy grinned feebly, admitting, "I guess I'm still on edge." He got up from the bench. "See you later."

Andy left the locker room and started for Hagerty's office, trying not to speculate too wildly on the reason for the summons. The door was open. It was a large room, expensively furnished with a deep rug on the floor. Hagerty was sitting behind his big mahogany desk wearing a baseball cap and a saggy sweat shirt. He looked out of place in the surroundings.

"Come in, Andy," he invited.

Andy stepped into the room, trying to appear as if he were accustomed to such visits. Hagerty gestured toward a chair, and Andy eased himself into it.

Hagerty smiled and said, "Relax. I'm not going to bite you."

Andy did the best he could to follow the instruction.

"You heard what happened down there in the locker room," the coach began abruptly.

Andy swallowed carefully and nodded, relieved to know the purpose of this powwow.

"I'm sorry, in one way, that it happened," went on Hagerty. "On the other hand, it's probably just as well to drag the thing out in the open." His eyes were fastened steadily on Andy when he fired the blunt question, "Do *you* have any doubts as to why your name was on that list?"

The question hit Andy like an unexpected tackle. He started an automatic denial of any such doubts, but the words got jammed together. He hesitated while he tried to get them straightened out, knowing that the hesitation was a virtual admission of guilt. It was too late, now, to run for cover. "I've almost *got* to wonder if I earned it, Coach," he blurted.

He fought against a sudden chill as the significance of his clumsy words came home to him. He saw an angry flare in the coach's eyes, then watched it fade. Hagerty grinned wryly.

"You almost made me mad," he said.

Andy's face was red and hot. "You ought to kick me out of here. I asked for it," he said.

The coach slowly shook his head. He looked at the ceiling for a while before saying, "I may not be the best football coach in the world, but at least I know what's going on around me. I know you're in a bad spot, Andy. I'd be stupid if I didn't know it. You've had it thrown in your teeth a lot of times by people like the jerk who sounded off down in the locker room. I, for one, can't blame you if your values sometimes get a little out of balance."

"I'm not proud of it," said Andy.

"In defense of myself," continued Hagerty, "I've got to make the point that, with me, football always comes first. There is no such thing as a head football coach who doesn't have a lot of pressure put on him from outside sources. I'm no stranger to it. If the time ever comes, however, when I let that pressure affect me against my better judgment, no one will have to ask for my resignation. Do you believe that, Andy?"

"Yes," said Andy, knowing that never in his life had he made a more truthful declaration.

"Are you certain then," persisted Hagerty, "that, even though you've got a lot to learn, I picked you for the squad because I believe you've got something I can use?"

"I'm certain of it, Coach."

"So much for that," said Hagerty. Then, as Andy started to get up, he added, "Hold on a minute." Andy sat back in his chair. "I understand you're a skin diver."

"Yes," Andy said, surprised. "I enjoy it."

"So far as I'm concerned you can take a whirl at it now and then if you want to."

Surprise still showed in Andy's face, so Hagerty went on to explain, "You're bound to build up a lot of tension on the football field, because I'm going to work you boys until you're dizzy. I've done a little scuba stuff, and I know how relaxing it can be. Sam Tedder's already talked to me about it, and I've given him permission."

"Well, thanks," said Andy gratefully. "I've sure missed it. And—and thanks, too, Coach, for putting me straight on the other thing."

"No charge," said Hagerty with a grin. "Go get your duds on."

Andy left the office feeling better than he had felt for some time. He had no way of knowing how long the feeling might last, but he determined to enjoy it while he could. He was certain of one thing, however. If Judd Hagerty should ask him to jump off a cliff, he would gladly do so.

CHAPTER
9

ANDY learned, during the next few days, that his previous football experience was mere kid stuff compared to the brand of football he now faced. Judd Hagerty, having made his final choice of players, was through fooling around with the fundamental tactics which had helped him make the choice. He drove the Pelicans without mercy as he ground their noses into the advanced science of the gridiron.

When the week end pulled around, Andy's brain was whirling with diagrams and football strategy. His muscles had the battered feel of having spent time in a cement mixer. He was more than ready for a scuba jaunt, eager for the soft cushion of the sea. Sam was equally enthusiastic over the prospect of breaking the football routine, and Andy hoped sincerely that Sam would meet the requirements of a diving companion.

Andy had been lucky during his freshman year. He had done most of his diving with a senior by the name of Barlow. Barlow, however, had graduated, posing

Andy with the problem of finding another underwater side-kick, a problem which Andy considered vitally important.

He was not afraid to go down alone—far from it. He had done so on occasions. He preferred, though, to observe strictly the first rule of skin diving—never dive alone. It was a sound rule, thoroughly practical, because the most experienced skin diver can run into trouble now and then, the sort of trouble in which another person can be mighty handy. It could mean the difference between an uneasy experience or a tragic one.

The right kind of diving companion was, therefore, essential from Andy's point of view, a person not only with experience, but, more important still, with the proper temperament. A man might have plenty of experience yet be inclined to take too many chances under the mistaken belief he was displaying bravery. It was a stupid way of showing off, because it saddled a companion with too much unnecessary responsibility. Andy never dove more than once with people of that type. The first dive would probably tell him what he had to know about Sam Tedder. Until then, he had to keep his fingers crossed.

They both breathed easier when the day dawned bright and clear, confirming the weather report of the previous afternoon. They treated themselves to the luxury of a long sleep in the morning, then went to the small yacht basin where Andy's boat, the *Tern,* was moored.

"Man, oh man, she's sure a beauty!" Sam approved.

Sam was not exaggerating. The *Tern* was a thirty-five-foot, twin-engine cabin cruiser, a flashy job displaying all the luxury which Jocko Baker believed should be associated with his name. He had justified himself with the assertion, "Nothing's too good for a son of mine."

"Yes," agreed Andy, "she's quite a craft. Dad wanted to give me something better, a real yacht, for instance. I finally convinced him that I only wanted it for skin diving, so he settled for this little twenty-five-thousand-dollar job with all the extras, ship-to-shore radio and so forth."

"You sound as if he had to twist your arm to make you take it," Sam said wonderingly.

"I guess I don't sound very grateful," confessed Andy, "even though the *Tern* is a mighty fine boat, and I like it a lot. It's just that—well, I can't help but think of it as a floating advertisement for Jocko Baker. It's certainly nothing that I've done anything to deserve."

"Tough luck," said Sam sadly. "Real tough luck." Then he added frankly, "I'd give an arm for a boat like this, but I'd probably feel the same as you do if I had one under these conditions. How fast is she?"

"Her twin-eights will kick her along over thirty miles an hour in the right kind of water."

"Whoosh!" said Sam. "I've handled a twin-engine job that belonged to a friend of mine, but it wasn't in this class. Who keeps the motors in shape?"

"I do," said Andy. "I'm pretty good at minor repairs. She hasn't been out for some time, but I've been coming down once a week to give the engines a short work-out. They're ready to roll."

They went below on a tour of inspection. Sam liked everything he saw, particularly the efficient, compact galley.

"Makes me hungry just to look at it," he said.

When they came back on deck, Sam asked casually, "No spear guns?"

Andy shook his head. "I don't go for them," he said. Then, as if trying to excuse himself, "I—well, it may sound sort of silly—I just don't like to kill fish, certainly not for the fun of it. When we go down there we're in their world, not ours. It belongs to them, and—well, I think there's something really beautiful about them, the way they move and all of that. I'd rather look at them than kill them."

Andy watched closely for a trace of criticism in Sam's expression. There was none. Sam nodded slowly, saying, "I guess I feel that way about it too. I've tried it, but I didn't like it. I didn't see an underwater camera in the cabin, either."

"I've got one," Andy said, "but I never had the patience to learn to use it properly. It's too technical for me. I'd rather just look and try to remember what I've seen."

Andy began to take the diving equipment from a locker. Inasmuch as Sam had had no time to charge his tank, it had been decided he would use Andy's gear for the day. Andy had three single tanks on board. He also owned his own compressor, which he kept in the small clubhouse of the Dolphin Diving Club.

Andy tested the tanks for pressure. They were all properly charged at 2200 pounds. He took two regulators from their padded boxes, handing one to Sam. He watched with interest as Sam deftly loosened the wing air yoke screw and removed the cork which protected the high-pressure valve. So far, so good. Sam seemed to know what he was doing.

"Better test, hadn't we?" said Sam. "They haven't been used for some time."

Andy nodded his approval. An occasional glance toward Sam was reassuring. Sam installed the regulator on the tank with the precise care necessary to protect the delicate mechanism. When he was certain it was seated properly, he opened the cylinder valve, then clamped his teeth around the mouthpiece. Andy went through the same procedure, and when assured that everything was working well, they removed the regulators to prevent possible damage from the motion of the boat.

"Weights?" asked Sam.

"Sure, here are the belts," said Andy, producing them. "How much?"

"About ten pounds."

"*Ten pounds?*" demanded Andy. "I only use four."

"I float like an empty barrel," Sam explained apologetically.

Andy provided Sam with a knife to slip into the

sheath on the weight belt. Sam had brought his own underwater watch and depth gauge. When everything had been checked, Andy started the motor, Sam cast off, and the *Tern* started smoothly into Tampa Bay.

"Have you got any place in mind?" asked Sam.

"Not particularly," said Andy. Then, after a moment, "There are several interesting old wrecks here in the bay. One of them has been authenticated as a Spanish ship, of the early seventeen hundreds, which was probably exploring up here through the Gulf."

"Any dirty old doubloons still lying around down there?" asked Sam with interest.

"It wasn't one of the treasure ships," said Andy. "Most of those which have been identified were wrecked on the east coast. There are still millions of dollars waiting there for anyone lucky enough to find it."

"Then what are we doing here?" demanded Sam.

"Skin diving," Andy reminded him.

"That's right. Almost forgot. Let's go see this Spanish ship."

"It's still possible to find stuff around these old wrecks," Andy said. "Of course hundreds of skin divers have already tried it, but underwater currents shift the sand around all the time, and every now and then something gets uncovered. It's a long shot, but it's fun to look."

Sam lounged in the cockpit, enjoying the soft air and sun. He was not inclined to talk too much, another thing which suited Andy fine. On jaunts of this sort Andy wanted to relax, to let the throb of the engine and the motion of the boat chase worries from his mind.

The peace of the moment was soon broken. Andy was watching the lazy soaring of a pelican when the bird suddenly changed course and headed toward the boat. For a moment Andy feared there might be a head-on collision, and there almost was. The foolhardy bird, accustomed enough to landing on stationary objects, was not so good at landing on the bow of a moving boat.

The bird was lucky. He managed to make some sort of contact with the forward deck, but his brakes failed. He ended up in a feathery scramble against the cabin, making sounds which could only be interpreted as bad language. Andy was relieved to see him get up, apparently intact, and stomp back to the bow of the boat where he nursed his outrage, trying to regain composure.

Sam had also watched the sloppy flying exhibition. Sam said, "They checked him out too soon on solo. Is he nuts or something?"

Andy did not answer right away. He was staring incredulously at the pelican. He announced finally, "Maybe *I'm* the one who's nuts. I think that's Mike!"

"Take it easy, son," Sam soothed. "That sun is mighty hot. You'd better put your hat on."

"I'm not kidding, Sam," said Andy earnestly. "I think it *is* Mike. Mike's got a dent in the right side of his beak, and this one's got a dent in the same place."

"Well, I'll be darned," Sam muttered, half-convinced.

"Take the wheel," said Andy.

Sam came to the bridge and assumed the steering job. Andy made his way along the narrow strip of deck between the cabin and the rail. He stopped when he reached the forward deck.

He said, "Hi, Mike. Welcome aboard."

The pelican cocked a baleful eye at him while Andy waited patiently. The big bird shook his feathers with an air of resignation. After a second shake he came toward Andy with a dignity that seemed to say, "Okay, I forgive you. Maybe it wasn't your fault after all." He came up to get his head scratched, dispelling all doubt of his identity. With the greeting over he returned to his place at the bow where he settled down like some strange figurehead.

Andy returned to the cockpit where Sam was still shaking his head in wonder. "It's not possible," he said. "It's got to be an accident. Either that, or he's got a built-in radar."

Andy shrugged helplessly, admitting, "It's got me licked, too. Anyway, it looks as if we've got a passenger."

Andy occupied himself now with some simple navigation. He got out a chart upon which he had made previous notes, having to do with time, direction, distance, and cross bearings from shore points. A short time later he shut off the motor.

"This should be close to the spot," he said. "We'll

probably have to scout around a bit, but we'll at least be under water."

Andy tossed the heavy, three-pronged anchor overboard after taking a hitch with the nylon anchor rope around the small capstan on the forward deck. Mike watched with interest.

Andy explained to Sam, "Sometimes the anchor gets hooked pretty solid to the bottom, and this gadget saves a lot of wear and tear on the back. All I have to do is to wind it up with this iron bar that fits into one of these holes. Okay, let's climb into our trunks and get started."

They changed in the cabin and came back on deck where they donned the scuba gear. Andy noted with approval that Sam adjusted the buckles with practiced fingers, doubling the webbed strap in such a manner that a quick yank on the projecting tab would instantly release the belt.

Andy said, "We might as well take these down too."

He produced a couple of self-inflating life preservers in small containers no larger than a cigarette pack. He then lowered the boarding ladder. As an added precaution he brought out a spare air tank and placed it on the cushions of the cockpit.

"Looks like we're all set," he said. "The wreck, if we can find it, is in about thirty feet of water, so we won't have to bother about decompressing on our way up. You ready?"

"You bet," said Sam. "All my diving has been in fresh water. There'll be a lot for me to see down here."

Sam started for the rail. Andy wondered if Sam

would jump into the water and risk dislodging his mask or other gear, but, here again, Sam showed further evidence of good underwater training. He backed slowly down the ladder and submerged slowly. At the last moment he inserted the mouthpiece, took several experimental breaths, then disappeared.

Andy went through the same procedure. Before gripping the mouthpiece in his teeth, he said politely to his guest, "So long, Mike. Don't get seasick."

CHAPTER
10

Once beneath the surface, Andy was in no hurry to do anything or to go anywhere, not until he had enjoyed, for several moments, the sheer delight of floating weightlessly, the almost painful satisfaction of entering a different world whose silence was a balm to nerves, where worries floated to the surface of the sea to leave him, temporarily anyway, at peace.

The lazy action of his flippers moved him slowly. Sam joined him, keeping pace, another healthy indication that, instead of mapping his own course, Sam was letting Andy call the shots. Andy briefly checked the rising bubbles from Sam's exhaling valve, noting that the breaths were evenly and normally spaced, as opposed to the irregular breaths beginners are sometimes inclined to take.

Andy led the way toward the bottom, curious to learn how accurately he had judged the spot of the old wreck. So far so good. At a depth of thirty feet he came

upon the sandy ledge upon which the wreck had settled, and while the two men coasted slowly along the
bottom Andy gathered another reassuring item about
Sam's underwater experience.

It was a small thing, but revealing. Sam came upon a
large conch shell, fluted, spiraled, and quite beautiful.
He reached out and picked it up. His fingers closed
upon it without hesitation, something that a beginner,
more than likely, would have failed to do, because water magnifies objects to one quarter larger than their
actual size. A beginner probably would have grabbed
too soon and missed. Sam held the shell for a moment
while he admired it, then reluctantly released it as the
two men went about their hunt.

They reached their goal much sooner than Andy had
anticipated. He realized that his navigation had, at
best, been more or less haphazard, and that nothing but
downright luck had brought him to the spot so soon.
It could easily have been far on the other side of the
anchored *Tern*.

Very little remained of the old galleon. Most of the
upper structure had long since disintegrated, leaving
some of the ribs, barnacle encrusted, reaching vainly
for the surface. There was a graceful pattern to these
durable monuments of wood which marked the final
resting place of daring men.

Andy had been here a few times before, but the spell
crept back on him again as his imagination probed the
past. Sam, too, seemed captured by the ghostly rem-
nants of high adventure. He remained motionless for

some time, his eyes sober behind the protective plastic of his mask.

The spell was broken by the arrival of a large grouper, strangely unafraid, who came within ten feet of them to study the intruders who had invaded his domain. He fastened them with a wall-eyed stare, and his big mouth moved as if he were actually forming words. Andy saw a burst of bubbles rise from Sam as he snorted in his mouthpiece with amusement. The bubbles scared the grouper, who flipped about and headed for a safer spot.

There was another brief diversion when Andy, glancing upward, saw an object floating above them in the water. He found it hard to believe, yet the hunch persisted that his friend, the pelican, was up there. Deciding to satisfy his curiosity, Andy called Sam's attention to the thing above, then started for the surface, rising slowly as he obeyed another safety rule—not to ascend faster than his bubbles. Sam joined him.

Andy's hunch was confirmed when he broke surface. It was Mike, all right, doing a little self-imposed guard duty. He bobbed his head as if in welcome, then shrugged his feathers as if to say, "Aw, shucks, I just happened to be here. How did *I* know you were down there?"

Andy, treading water, removed his mouthpiece, careful to keep it above the water. Sam also removed his. "He followed us sure as anything," said Andy, puzzled. "I wonder how he managed it."

"Sonar?" suggested Sam. Then, seriously, "I really

believe that fool bird is trying to take care of you. He looks worried."

Andy laughed, unable, however, to deny Sam's statement. If a pelican could look worried, Mike was certainly accomplishing it as he fixed an accusing eye on Andy. The look said, "What in thunder are you doing down there with the fish? Why don't you stay up where you belong?"

"I'm sorry, Mike," Andy apologized. "I'll try to explain later. Right now we're busy."

Andy inserted his mouthpiece, arched his body in a surface dive, and started back toward the bottom. Sam followed. Once down there Andy set the search example by scooping with his hands at the irregular mounds of loose sand, which looked as if they might conceal something interesting.

He realized, of course, that the chances of finding anything important were virtually nonexistent, but the fun of exploration would be lost if he conceded this too strongly. It was better to pretend that something had been overlooked by other divers, or that the shifting sand had worked some ancient relic toward the surface where a probing hand might find it. Sam, he noted, had quickly caught the spirit of the thing. His big hands were scooping with enthusiasm.

Andy suddenly caught sight of something at the base of one of the big ribs which curved upward from the sand. He moved in cautiously beneath an adjoining rib, careful not to touch the barnacles which could easily cause nasty cuts. When he reached the object he had spotted, it appeared to be a metal bar of some sort, pitted and corroded by the sea. He gave it a tentative wiggle. It was solid.

He started to tunnel under it, finding it slow work because the loose sand would not co-operate. He made some headway, though, enough to increase his interest when he began to feel some motion in the bar. He worked slowly in order to keep his breathing normal and to conserve his air. When he was finally able to slide his hand beneath the bar, he recognized what it was immediately. It did not amuse him as it should have done. The thing he felt was a more or less modern T-joint. He had been wasting his excitement and his energy on a length of plumbing pipe.

A flare of angry petulance caused Andy, at this point, to make a serious blunder. He gave the pipe a violent jerk. It suddenly came loose, and the things that happened next were in the nature of a chain reaction. His body, lurching backward, caused his tank to come in jarring contact with the rib behind him, and the rib, undoubtedly worn thin at a point beneath the sand, came down on top of him.

Andy felt the solid settling of its weight before he could move clear. Wild panic hit him like a blow as he felt himself pushed slowly and relentlessly into the sand. His first useless struggles were instinctive. He promptly checked them, however, when he forced his mind to a fundamental underwater law—don't lose your head. He was in a bad jam and he knew it. Panic would only make things worse. It would waste his precious air supply.

Sam, as yet, had not noticed his predicament. It gave Andy time to pull himself together, a condition he accomplished sooner than he had dared to hope. He made himself relax, and, once assured he was not injured, he put his brain to work. The rib, fortunately, was resting on the tank, protecting him from barnacles. It was a huge relief, also, to see Sam coming toward him.

Sam's attitude was reassuring. He studied the situation carefully, with no show of panic. He took out his knife and began to clear the barnacles from a spot on the underside of the curving rib. He then placed his shoulder on the spot and threw his huge strength into the job of lifting. The rib trembled, nothing more. The sand was too loose to give him sufficient purchase with his feet.

Once convinced that further effort would be useless he came around to squat in front of Andy. He touched Andy's watch, then the tank. Andy got the message. Surprised at his own calmness, he computed swiftly before opening and closing his hand three times to indicate he had approximately fifteen minutes of air left, including the five-minute reserve supply. Sam nodded. He made motions saying he would bring down the reserve tank.

Andy also nodded; then, as an idea burst into his mind, he restrained Sam from hurrying to the surface. Sam watched attentively while Andy pantomimed with all the talent he could muster. He pointed in the direction of the *Tern,* then made a circular motion with his hand, trying to tell Sam that the *Tern's* capstan was capable of lifting a heavy weight. Sam nodded, understanding. Andy then pointed straight above before making a flapping gesture with his hands, suggesting that Mike the pelican, if still faithful to his post, would lead the *Tern* back to the spot above the wreck.

Sam left Andy to an agony of waiting. There were moments when he wondered if the discipline he had imposed upon himself would crack. He could not look upward to see if Mike were still on duty. He could only hope. He tried to keep from looking at his watch, finding it impossible to keep his eyes away. He fought against another tremor of panic as he switched to his emergency supply of air. Five minutes left.

He choked back a sob of gratitude when he heard the *Tern's* propeller noise. It seemed hours, rather than seconds, when he saw the anchor coming down. Sam was lowering it carefully on the off chance of hitting Andy. It came down some fifteen feet away, a credit to Sam's calculations and to Mike's loyalty.

Sam followed the anchor promptly, wearing the full tank of air. His movements, restricted by the density of the water, seemed discouragingly slow to Andy, yet he knew that Sam was working rapidly under the conditions. He wrapped the stout anchor rope securely around the rib. He filled his lungs before jerking the release tabs of his harness. He gave the full tank to

Andy, flashed a reassuring grin, and headed for the surface.

The wait, this time, was considerably easier. Andy made the change to his new air supply by raising the mouthpiece above his head until bubbles emerged, then placing it swiftly in his mouth. Everything depended now upon the *Tern*'s small capstan and upon the strength of the nylon rope.

When the rope began to tighten, it was hard for Andy not to disobey another diving law—don't hold your breath. The suspense, almost unbearable, was mercifully brief. The old rib shuddered, resisted stubbornly, then gradually began to rise. Andy forced himself to wait until he knew the rib was clear. He moved fast, then, scrambling across the sand like a frightened crab. Once free, he took a moment to compose himself. When his breathing became reasonably normal, he cradled the spare tank in his arms and started for the surface.

He discarded the mouthpiece when his head came out. He gulped a few lungfuls of the fresh air with the grateful manner of a man who had begun to doubt that he would ever enjoy such air again. By the time he had climbed on deck, however, his gratitude had changed to anger.

"Of all the stupid idiots I ever heard of," he burst out, "I top the list! It takes a self-made moron to get in that sort of jam. Andy Baker knows all there is to know about skin diving. He yaks about underwater safety to anybody who will listen to him, then goes down and pulls the dumbest thing a diver ever pulled. You should have left me down there."

Sam considered this a moment before saying, "Mike wouldn't have liked it."

Andy muttered a few more uncomplimentary things about himself. Sam let him get it all out of his system, recognizing it for what it was, a blowoff to relieve an overdose of strain. When Andy finally ran down he steadied himself with another deep breath.

"Thanks, Sam," he said belatedly.

Sam was donning the full tank of air. He sidetracked any further show of gratitude by saying, "Better thank Mike, too. He stayed right on the job."

Accepting the cue, Andy tossed a brief salute to Mike, who had taken his position once more on the bow. Mike modestly ignored the gesture. He wiggled his tail to convey the message, "Aw, shucks, it was nothing, really. I did it for a pal."

Sam, preparing to go over the side, said, "Be back in a minute, soon as I unwind the anchor rope."

During the short time Sam was gone, Andy had a chance to catalogue the few things he had learned so recently. To start with, he would never again be smug about his ability to take care of himself under water. He would try, of course, to be more careful in the future, but this was no assurance that the unexpected would not happen. The first rule of diving—don't go down alone—was more firmly implanted in his mind than ever. Had he been down this time alone, the ghosts of the old galleon would have had some company. He was also able to discard whatever doubts he had held about Sam Tedder as a diving companion. Sam was a good guy to have around.

A surprise awaited them when they returned to the yacht basin. A new boat had been moored in one of the slips, a big elaborate cabin cruiser, which Andy judged to be at least a forty footer. He assumed it was a transient, belonging to some wealthy parent visiting a son or daughter at the university.

The assumption was destroyed when the *Tern* drew closer. Mark Sutton paced the deck with an air of ownership, strutting about while a group of students on the pier admired the craft.

"Well, well, well," said Sam. "Our boy Mark seems to be trying to crash the big league. I knew he'd been taking skin-diving lessons, but why does he need that ocean liner for the job?"

"It figures," said Andy, grinning. "His pop, Tex Sutton, is trying to rub it in to my pop, and Mark, for some reason he seems to think important, is trying to rub it into me. Bigger and better, that's the motto, so they hustle out and get a bigger boat."

The *Tern*, by this time, was in hailing distance. Mark bawled in his best sea-going style, "Watch yourself there, Skipper! Don't ram that scow into the dock!"

The warning was unnecessary. Andy brought the *Tern* deftly into the slip beside Mark's boat. While Sam stepped out to secure the mooring lines, Mark waited for some comment from Andy.

Andy studied the other boat with interest before asking, "Are you going into the passenger business, Mark?"

Mark turned red. Andy was not reacting properly. To complicate things even more for Mark, Andy's amusement was so completely genuine that it blocked off any chance for Mark to gloat. It put him in a bad spot, too, with the watchers on the pier.

Andy, with a dramatic sense of timing, which might have been inherited from his father, moved off stage before Mark could think of anything to say. Andy descended to the cabin as if he had several things to do in order to leave the *Tern* shipshape. Mark was not in sight when he came out.

On the way home, Sam observed, "Lovable character, isn't he?"

"Charming," agreed Andy. "I wish he'd keep out of my hair."

"He won't," said Sam.

Andy agreed again, "I'm afraid you're right."

CHAPTER

11

Judd Hagerty maintained the swift, relentless pace of daily practice. He displayed a touch of genius in his knowledge of the men he worked with. He seemed to sense each man's capacity, the limit of his ability to learn and the limit of his ability to absorb the knocks. He pushed each individual to this limit, but never into the dangerous area beyond.

The Pelicans, for the most part, took it all without complaint, a tribute, in itself, to their confidence in Hagerty. There were, of course, a few dissenters. No football team would be complete without them, but these few men who believed they were being worked too hard without proper recognition soon learned to keep their gripes unspoken in the presence of the other men whose loyalty to Hagerty was unquestioning and solid.

The football material, so far as Andy could determine, was reasonably good. He had no basis for comparison in his own experience, but several of the

Pelican veterans seemed cautiously assured that Hagerty could put a strong team on the field. The trick would be to keep it strong, because the Pelican bench could not be relied on with too much confidence. It was largely composed of men with fine potentials but without enough experience. In another year these same men might be formidable. This year, unfortunately, was the one that counted.

Gradually Andy realized just how much this year counted, and the extent of its importance was alarming. He absorbed the feeling from the other Pelicans, particularly from the veterans whose long association with Judd Hagerty had built a strong affection for the coach. These men set the pace, batting their brains out like fanatics, determined to prove beyond all doubt that Hagerty was the best coach in the league, a resolve which spread like a contagious virus through the other members of the team.

The feeling received stimulus from an outside source —a critical, pessimistic element in the student body whose attitude drove the Pelicans to greater efforts. The disgraceful incident of the effigy was not repeated. On the other hand, it was not forgotten. It still rankled in the minds of some, and was still tacitly approved by others, those who insisted on nursing their resentment at the Pelicans' poor showing of the previous year.

The condition was not entirely the students' fault. Those who chose to believe along these lines had outside help. Their sentiments might possibly have been diverted in the opposite direction by the proper kind of outside help. Unfortunately, in this case, news was news. The sports reporters had their orders to dig up stuff on football, and when the great alumnus speaks his mind it has to be considered news. Jocko Baker sounded off again.

A St. Petersburg sports writer reported in his column:

Mr. Jocko Baker is still firm in the belief that Gulf football should be improved. Mr. Baker stated, "I don't want anyone to get me wrong. I don't want to appear in the role of a bull-headed alumnus who wants to stir up trouble just for the fun of it. I want to let the record speak for itself—the Pelican football record, and I think I'm safe in saying that it hasn't spoken very loudly for the past two years. Gulf University has established itself as a first-class football school, and a lot of us have expended considerable effort and expense to help it reach that goal. Do we want to stay up there, or do we want to hit the skids? It's as simple as that. The answer is in the hands of the Board of Directors and the Athletic Department."

When asked the direct question, "Do you believe that Judd Hagerty should be removed from the position of head coach?" Mr. Baker replied, "No, I don't think that Hagerty should be replaced—not if he can give us a winning team. If he can't," Mr. Baker shrugged, "we'll have to make our decision for the good of the school. I use the word *we*, because my opinion is shared by other Gulf alumni—influential men. Unfortunately, I have been placed in the unpopular role of spokesman."

The article appeared in an afternoon paper. Andy did not see it until he and Sam returned from dinner at the training table. They were together in Andy's room. Sam read it first. His face went stiff and blank.

"What gives?" demanded Andy, feeling a swift chill of apprehension.

Sam shrugged, handing the paper to Andy. "Your dad," said Sam by way of preparation.

Andy read the column swiftly. He sat for several moments, his anger struggling with shame. He finally burst out, "Why can't he keep his big mouth shut?"

"He probably thinks he's doing the right thing," said Sam without conviction.

"Nuts!" said Andy violently. "He only thinks of Jocko Baker! He needs publicity like a pig needs food, and he gets it any way he can. I sometimes wish that—that—" he clamped his teeth upon the words, concluding weakly, "what's the use?"

Sam sat in unhappy silence, suffering with Andy. Andy shook himself at last and said resignedly, "I hate to feel that way about my father."

Sam commented mildly, "I must say you don't have much in common."

"The understatement of the year," said Andy, managing a weak grin. "What happens now?"

Sam shrugged again. "I sort of hate to think."

"But look," protested Andy hopefully. "Why should anyone pay attention to what *he* says?"

Sam considered this for a moment before saying thoughtfully, "I don't think it makes an actual differ-

ence what Jocko Baker himself says, it's just that someone with a lot of weight to swing has come out and *said*
it. You know what college students are like, a restless
bunch with half-baked theories who are always looking
around for something to make an issue of, and most of
them don't care much what the issue is."

"I'll buy that," said Andy.

"Most of us think we're a lot smarter than we are,"
continued Sam, "and those who think they're the smart-
est are generally the ones who can be led around by the
nose. There are a lot like that around, I'm sorry to say."

"In other words, that loyal alumnus, Jocko Baker,
has started to stir up a mess."

"The mess was started some time ago," Sam reminded him, "when someone had the bright idea of
stringing up that effigy."

"I know," said Andy wearily. "And now, with some
encouragement from Jocko, they'll probably think
about stringing up another. It could happen any day
now."

Jocko's blowoff presented Andy with a personal
problem of considerable size—the job of facing the
other Pelicans. How would they accept the man whose
father seemed determined to torpedo the entire squad?
He braced himself for the occasion, only to find, with
huge relief, that the precaution was unnecessary.

The Pelicans' attitude toward him was strained, but
not in the manner he had feared it might be. Their attempts at casualness might have been amusing had the
situation been less serious. The overtures were over-

done and unintentionally clumsy, but the message came through clear and strong. By carefully avoiding all mention of the ticklish subject, they were telling him, as best they could, that he was still a Pelican and that Jocko's statement had not changed a thing in their relations with his son.

Mark Sutton kept looking for an opening, his harpoon poised and ready, but when an opening refused to show itself he used his head and kept his mouth shut. Andy sensed all this as he assumed his own brand of casualness, trying not to let his gratitude be too apparent. It was a fine moment in his life, one he would not soon forget.

Andy learned during the next few days that his pessimistic forecast of another effigy party was exaggerated. The effect of Jocko's statement on the student body was not of an explosive quality, it was more like the relighting of a fuse which, if allowed to burn, might finally reach the powder barrel. The subdued sizzling of the fuse could be heard in several campus groups.

A taut excitement gripped the school, an excitement which had selected its own climactic moment—the Pelicans' first game of the season to be played on their own field against Palmetto College from the Florida east coast. The climax was established entirely by public sentiment, which whipped itself into the conviction that the game against Palmetto was the big payoff, a showdown that would give the critics all the proof they needed, one way or another. The fairness of the matter did not enter the decision. The fans wanted it that way, and that was that. They anticipated all the drama such a game would spread before them. It was easy, therefore, for the fans to believe that such a game was more important than it actually was.

Hagerty was quick to sense the danger of the emotional jag the students were enjoying. He pointed out their fallacy of reasoning to the Pelicans. They nodded in solemn understanding. They agreed entirely with their coach. They tried their best to fight against the fever, but it crept into their veins. They tried to believe that the Palmetto game was just a warm-up for the bigger games to come, but the constant hammering of the fans made them begin to believe that the future of Judd Hagerty might hang upon the outcome of this game, that they held their coach's future in their hands.

The football practices were grim affairs in the week preceding the Palmetto battle. Hagerty worked desperately to keep the men relaxed, not getting very far with the attempt. Andy found himself as hot-eyed and determined as the rest, even though his chance of getting in the game was slim. He became obsessed like all the other Pelicans with the urge to roll up an overwhelming score against the Palmetto Gulls.

Palmetto was a relatively small school as compared with Gulf. Their football team was in the building stage, yet, even though football was a number one priority, they had not yet reached the point of threatening the larger schools. That is to say, they had not reached that point the previous year. The Pelicans, despite admitted weakness, had smacked the Gulls down 21-6.

This year the Pelicans intended to make the spread a whole lot wider.

The usual pre-game scare stories seeped in from the enemy camp to start the customary war of nerves. They had a sophomore halfback, Archie Tragg, who, so went the report, was dynamite on legs. A sophomore end, Stu Dover, was supposed to be as hot as a blowtorch. The Gulls were talking big.

"And you'd better listen to them," Hagerty warned the Pelicans. "You've been licking your chops as if getting ready for a turkey dinner. Don't figure these Gulls for pushovers even if we *do* outweigh them in the line. They could be tough."

The Pelicans nodded agreement. They did not exchange glances until the coach's back was turned. The glances said, "We'll tear 'em limb from limb!"

Andy wondered, now and then, why he was allowing himself to get so steamed up about the opening game, a game in which he did not expect to play. He had disciplined himself to accept the role of third-string substitute, and was sensible enough to realize, without resentment, that that was where he belonged. He was satisfied to know he had improved daily during practice, and was assured he would continue to improve. It was not easy for him to admit that Mark Sutton was still more reliable and experienced at right half, the spot for which Andy was being groomed. Andy managed to accept it, though, because it was the truth. It appeared that Mark would share the duties in this spot with Joe Jasper, one of the veterans.

There was very little pre-game hoopla as the day approached. The campus did not blossom with placards reading, *Beat the Gulls*. The fans regarded a mere victory over the Gulls as unimportant and assumed the Pelicans would win. The issue was not victory, it was the manner of the victory, its impressiveness or its failure to impress.

It was inevitable, of course, that Jocko Baker should be present at this all-important opening game, a game which he had forced to be so all-important. The great man, naturally, would have to be there to impose judgment, and to hand down his decision. He could do no less for his beloved alma mater.

Andy did not look forward to his father's visit. As usual, he regretted his resentment, but there was nothing he could do about it except to hope that someday things might be different. His meeting with Jocko on the day before the game was marked by its customary strain, but fortunately not by friction. Jocko studiously avoided mention of the football situation.

The following day, though fine for football, was not so fine for Andy when it turned out that his participation in the opening game might be even more inglorious than he had anticipated. Before he had a chance to get into his togs, the student football manager, Milt Penny, approached him in the locker room. Milt seemed in quite a dither—also a bit embarrassed.

He said, "Look, Andy, can I talk to you a minute?"

"Sure," said Andy without caution. "What can I do for you?"

"I'm glad you put it that way," Milt said gratefully. "You can do a lot for me."

Andy began to sense his choice of words had been a little careless. With more reserve he asked, "What is it?"

"I'm in a bind," confessed Milt nervously. "I goofed up. You can help me."

"How?"

"It's about our mascot, Mike the pelican."

A belated chill of apprehension laid its hand on Andy's spine. He liked Milt Penny. Milt was a good manager who worked like a mule and batted his brains out for the welfare of the Pelicans. He hated to let Milt down, but there was something truly menacing about Milt's words.

"Go on," said Andy.

"It's like this," said Milt with almost babbling eagerness. "It's one of my jobs to get Mike out to all the games, and this game in particular. This is my first year as manager, and—well, with all the other excitement, I just plain forgot."

"Where is Mike now?" asked Andy, getting in deeper.

"We're lucky, mighty lucky. He's out in his pond."

"Okay," said Andy practically. "Go get him and take him out."

"You don't understand," said Milt miserably. "I can't get near him, and as soon as he hears the first yell out of the crowd he'll be halfway to South America. He hates football."

"How did they get him out to the field in other years?"

"We played him dirt. We tricked him into a cage a couple of days ahead of time. Then they took him to the field in the cage. It took four men to get him out and hooked up to his perch."

"But why pick on me?"

"Everybody knows the bird is nuts about you, Andy. He'll do anything you want him to."

"Then you want me to be the sneaky jerk who gets him in the cage for you."

"It's worse than that," said Milt. "We can't find the cage. I'm asking you, Andy, as a big favor to me, and—" with belated reverence he added—"to the school, to lead him out there and chain him to his perch."

"Oh, no!" groaned Andy.

"And you'd better go out right now," suggested Milt, gaining confidence. "You can tie him down before he turns yellow and deserts. You can take him out to the field later."

Andy pretended to give the matter thought, knowing all the while that he was trapped. He let Milt squirm a while.

He finally said, "You're hitting below the belt, but I guess all managers learn that while they're still young. You can stop crying now. I'll take care of Mike."

"Thanks, Andy," said Milt huskily. "Thanks a lot. Your grateful school will list you among its heroes. And here," he said, grinning, "are the leg irons."

He reached in his pocket and drew out a light chain fastened to a metal leg band. Andy took the chain, then made an impulsive move to wrap it around Milt's neck, a move sincere enough to cause Milt quick alarm. He backed away in haste.

At a safe distance he said, "Thanks again," and hurried off to other duties.

Andy went out to make a prisoner of Mike, hoping earnestly that Mike would put up such a fight that Andy would be justified in letting him escape. Mike's submission, however, was discouraging. He permitted Andy to secure the leg band and to fasten the chain to a small tree, co-operating with a sad air of disillusionment. His forlorn croak conveyed the message, "You can't even trust a pal." Andy felt like a heel.

He also felt like a fool when the time came to lead Mike to the field. Mike regarded Andy's football togs with prompt alarm, then paid him the tribute of accepting him even as a football player. They started off, but Mike, though willing, had trouble with the chain. He kept getting his feet tangled in it.

Andy, in exasperation, said, "You clumsy clown!"

Mike cocked an accusing eye at him, replying, in effect, "What did you expect, a ballet dancer?"

Andy sighed resignedly. "Okay," he said, "let's try it this way."

He gingerly lifted Mike off the ground, expecting the worst. The pelican did not object. On the contrary, when Andy tucked him beneath his arm like an oversize football Mike relaxed contentedly as if to say, "Why didn't we think of this before?"

The ordeal of entering the field was still ahead, and Andy began to sweat a little at the thought of appearing in this fashion. Most of the fans were already in their seats, thousands of them, many more than ordinarily showed up for an opening game, and suddenly the unnerving thought hit Andy that his dad would be among them.

Yes, Jocko Baker would be there, sitting in a choice seat on the fifty-yard line. He would be waiting proudly for his only son and heir to make his first appearance in the football uniform of his alma mater. He had waited many years for this important moment, the day when his son would trot upon the field with spring in his legs and courage in his heart. Instead, his son would plod upon the field carrying a pelican.

Andy could picture the expression on his father's face, the stricken look of a man stabbed in the back, the horror of having his huge ego punctured like a balloon, and suddenly the picture pleased Andy as few pictures could have done. He suffered, it is true, a brief feeling of disloyalty, a feeling overpowered by the fitness of the situation.

Jocko Baker, master of the wisecrack, was supposedly a connoisseur of comedy, yet none of Jocko's high-paid writers could come up with anything like this, with all its subtle undertones. To start with they would not have dared to manufacture a routine with Jocko on the receiving end of a monumental gag. It tickled Andy's fancy. It made his entrance to the field distinctive rather than undignified. He grinned with wide enjoyment while the crowd gave him an enthusiastic hand.

As he made his way toward Mike's perch at the end

of the bench he tried to spot his father, not wanting to miss any part of Jocko's reaction to the scene. Jocko was not in the fifty-yard-line box that he reserved throughout the season. His satellites were there, but not the boss.

Andy experienced a brief moment of disappointment before seeing that his father had taken advantage of an important person's privilege. Jocko was on the field, standing near the bench in a group of coaches, officials, and other important people. He was expansive, entertaining them with words and gestures. When he found that someone was stealing the show from him he glanced resentfully toward Andy, then took a double take. One of his gestures halted in mid-action to freeze him in the position of a mannequin whose arms have been clumsily arranged. Andy was close enough to watch the shock of horror quiver through his father's bulk.

Jocko, however, was a veteran of profound experience. Sensitive to audience reaction, he was not the sort of man to be easily upstaged without mounting a prompt counterattack. In this instance, though, he was smart enough to understand that Mike and Andy were formidable foes. They were dominating the show, so Jocko wisely fell back on the old, effective tactic—if you can't lick 'em, join 'em. He whisked away his shocked expression with professional agility. He substituted a convincing smile of welcome.

"Well, well, son," he boomed, "I see you've just brought us a new quarterback."

"Not Mike," said Andy with a grin. "He's too smart to get his brains beat out in football."

"He's got a point there," agreed Jocko heartily.

Andy felt some warning twitches traveling through Mike, a message indicating that Mike had just included hearty people in the long list of things he hated. It seemed sensible, at this point, to place Mike on the ground before his hasty temper took control. Andy eased him gently to his feet, keeping a firm grip on the chain. Mike shook his feathers into place, then cocked a glance at Andy which said grudgingly, "Thanks for the ride, pal." A beady stare at Jocko added testily, "But get this fat character out of my sight before I forget my manners."

Jocko, however, was in no hurry to leave. It was a matter of principle. He timed his fatherly chat just long enough to convince the fans that he was delighted to see his son, even though Andy had carried a pelican instead of a football on the field.

Having assured himself that he had convinced the crowd, Jocko made two tactical blunders. The first was his failure to convince Mike. The second, and more serious, was his failure to back off from the scene. He turned abruptly, presenting Mike with one of the largest, most inviting targets he had seen for days, and Mike, the opportunist, simply had to take advantage of it.

There was enough slack in the chain to give Mike all the room he needed. His attack, though probably cowardly, was masterful—an expert at his best. Andy's yell of warning and his frantic jerk upon the chain came a fraction of a second late. When Mike made connection there was nothing artificial about Jocko's whoop of pain. It was insisted later, by the track coach, that no man of equal size could have bettered Jocko's record for the hop, step, and jump.

The fans broke loose. They loved it. Never in his spectacular career had Jocko Baker afforded so much hilarity to so many people. It put him on a spot, but, trooper that he was, he wiggled out of it, because instinct prompted him to prolong the laughter if he could. He produced a hankerchief before he lost momentum. He waved it frantically as a white token of surrender while he clowned his way into the box. Andy noted that his father sat down very gingerly. Andy tried hard to regret the incident, finding the effort more than he could manage.

He turned on Mike, demanding sternly, "Aren't you ashamed of yourself? You hoodlum!"

Mike ignored him with an air of, "I don't answer stupid questions."

With Mike in his present frame of mind, Andy anticipated trouble when he tried to put him on the perch. His apprehension proved he still had things to learn about the bird. Mike settled on the perch with no complaint at all—the most contented, smuggest pelican in Florida.

CHAPTER
12

THE fans recovered quickly from the unexpected entertainment. They sank into a somber mood of watchful waiting. Andy, though unfamiliar with football crowds, sensed something strange in this one. It was almost as if they were on hand to watch an execution rather than a football game. Andy felt his skin creep as he joined his teammates for the pre-game warm-up.

He had a chance to say to Sam, "Is my imagination playing tricks on me, or is this crowd acting funny?"

"There's nothing wrong with your imagination," Sam assured him. "They're sitting there like buzzards in a tree."

The other Pelicans also seemed aware of the fans' unnatural tension. Their glances toward the crowd were varied. Some were angry, some contemptuous, others worried. Invariably, however, they went back to practice with unnecessary violence. Andy hoped this was a good sign. He could not be sure.

The Palmetto rooters had crossed the state in a cavalcade of buses. They were there in force, and their attitude contrasted sharply with the behavior of the Pelican rooters. The noise they made was healthy, challenging, and definitely cocky. This was a vitally important game to them. They were there to watch their team play football, not to sit in judgment on their coach's future.

The Gulls' practice session was something to claim attention—which it did. The Pelicans, as if impelled against their better judgment, kept sneaking critical glances toward the Gulls, and the Gulls put on a show. They ran their signals in precise, swift patterns. They put an explosive quality into their formations, more, it seemed, than was necessary for an ordinary warm-up. Andy got the firm impression that the drill had been carefully rehearsed for the benefit of the Pelicans, and that the show of speed and vinegar was having the desired effect. The Pelicans tried to match the Gulls' performance, a mistake which threw their timing out of gear.

Hagerty's pre-game instructions to the team were brief. "I've tried to convince you," he began, "that this game is not as important as you have been led to believe. You've been played for suckers. You've been victims of an artificial build-up. You've swallowed the idiotic hokum that the outcome of this game will be an omen which will govern the other games ahead of us. That's a lot of bunk."

He stopped for a moment, letting his eyes travel around the group. "I know why this game seems so important to you. I'd be a fool if I didn't know, and, believe me, I appreciate your concern as well as what you're trying to do for me. It's a great satisfaction for me to know this. On the other hand, it's a disappointment to me to feel that my brand of coaching has failed to keep your minds on football and on nothing else but football.

"My usual advice, as some of you already know, is to think of one game at a time, the one you're playing. Today, however, I'm asking you to believe that the games ahead of us will be equally important, maybe more so, than the game today. Try to play the kind of football that you and I know you *can* play. Don't, for goodness' sake, try to play any better than that."

Andy was assured that Hagerty had done as good a job as any coach could have done to relieve the unnatural tension of the Pelicans, yet, when the team started for the field, Andy could still sense the feverish, strained quality of the Pelicans' mood. They were almost like soldiers going into battle, keyed up by the final warning, "If the enemy gets beyond this point, the war is lost."

Andy wore a worried frown as he took his place on the bench. He could still cling, however, to the hope that Hagerty's apprehension might be exaggerated, that the Pelicans, after all, might be in the proper frame of mind to do what they were planning to do—roll up a formidable score against the Gulls.

If the Gulls had any fear along this line it was not apparent when they took the field. They pranced out with a confidence which seemed genuine. Having won the toss, they had elected to receive, another indication they had faith in their offensive and did not intend to bog down and be forced to kick from deep in their own territory.

Ralph Hopper, Pelican fullback, got his toe into a fine kick down the center of the field. Archie Tragg was there to take it inside the ten-yard line. He held back to let his interference form, but the Gull blockers had little chance to spring their speedy back into the open.

The Pelicans, with speed of their own, came hurtling wild-eyed down the field, putting everything they had saved for days into the savageness of their attack. They blasted through the Gulls like a tornado through a haystack. They scattered the interference handily to pile Tragg up on the fourteen-yard line.

A happy, surprised yell came from the Pelican fans. Andy unclenched his fists and breathed again. He allowed himself a cautious surge of optimism, trying to believe that the Pelicans were, after all, in the proper frame of mind, that their fanatic kickoff charge might actually foretell the pattern of the game. His glance at Hagerty revealed nothing. There was no expression of approval on the coach's face.

The Gulls displayed no great alarm at the way they had been tossed around. Their retreat into the huddle was orderly and businesslike. They broke fast from the huddle and hurried to the line. The Pelicans, taut as sprinters on their marks, were poised to strike again.

Jeff Mobry, Pelican right tackle, jumped the gun, to make contact with an opposing lineman. The five-yard off-side penalty was a present for the Gulls.

Their quarterback, Tom Garson, pulled them back into another huddle. It was a light team but a fast one. Pre-season information, all that was available, pegged the Gulls as a passing and wide-running team. The Pelicans decided to counter this, temporarily at least, with a 7-1-2-1 defense, which was based on the theory that the full seven-man line, heavier and stronger than the opposing linemen, could crash into the Gull backfield in time to break up the passes or the end runs. If this formation proved ineffective, it could quickly be shifted into a six-man line or even a five-man line, whichever was considered necessary for the best defense, a lot of which depended on what plays the Gulls threw at them.

When the Gulls hurried from their huddle, the Pelicans were poised, hot-eyed, to meet them and to chew them up. The play broke fast with the Gulls sending a screen of interference toward right end. Garson faked a hand-off to his right half who followed the blockers. Hobb Kemper, Pelican right tackle, went storming into the Gull backfield like a rampaging buffalo. He broke up the end run with a mighty tackle, learning too late that the man he tackled did not have the ball. The ball carrier was Archie Tragg, who flashed unhindered through the big hole Kemper had so graciously left for him.

Sam Tedder as a line-backer, managed, after a long

lunge, to slap a big hand against Tragg's leg with power enough to throw Tragg momentarily off balance. If Sam had missed, Tragg might have gone the distance. As it was, Ding Kibby, the quarterback, had time to come from his deep spot to hold Tragg to an eight-yard gain. The Gulls now had running room with the ball on their twenty-seven-yard line.

Andy, despite the bad scare the Gulls had given him, was grudgingly forced to admire Tom Garson's choice of an opening play. He had caught the Pelicans flat-footed by sending the play into the Pelican line, a forward wall which, in theory, should be able to contain the Gulls' power plays. There was evidence, too, that Garson had spotted the Pelicans' overeagerness and had used it to his advantage, an early warning which the Pelicans should heed by pegging Garson as an alert and cagey quarterback.

He gave prompt evidence of this. The Pelicans had been played for suckers, and were obviously peeved and temporarily befuddled by the dirty trick the Gulls had played on them. Garson gave them no time to recover. The Gull huddle was a fast one, and the play got under way with swift precision.

Garson gambled a little by calling a screen pass deep in his own territory. He faked Tragg into the weak side of the line, but the Pelicans were not too badly fooled by the maneuver. They stormed into the Gull backfield with a ferocity which could have been more effective had it been a little less ferocious. As it was, the Pelicans grabbed at everything that moved, which was not a good idea, because some of the moving Gulls were not important to the play. The Pelicans displayed an awesome show of power which looked rather silly in comparison to the smooth co-ordination of the Gulls.

Garson, after the fake belly pass, flipped the ball to his other halfback, Ray Minty, who was angling toward the side line. Minty gathered in the ball, side-stepped the frantic grab of a Pelican lineman, then moved in behind the screen which was picking off the Pelican defenders.

It was Sam Tedder again who broke up the interference. He could move his huge bulk, for a short distance, with amazing speed. He got across in time to wipe out a pair of Gulls who had made the mistake of running too close together. Ding Kibby came in from his safety spot to nail the ball carrier with a hasty but effective tackle near the side line. The ball squirted from the Gull's hands before he hit the ground. It rolled playfully up the field for five more yards, then, as if drawn by a magnet, dribbled out of bounds to leave the Gulls still in possession of the ball. The over-all gain was sixteen yards.

It was a hard jolt for any team to absorb, particularly for an overwrought team like the Pelicans. The running gain was bad enough, but the unearned extra yardage from a fumble made things even worse. The situation was not helped much by the Pelican fans. Most of them were shocked to silence, a silence which permitted several protests to come through loud and clear. One of these jarred roughly upon Andy's ears.

"Wake up, you clowns! Let's see some football!"

They were not exactly words expected from a loyal fan, decided Andy. They sent a quiver of anger up his spine. He shot a glance at Hagerty, who sat immobile, poker faced. He merely nodded brief approval when Ding Kibby called time out to give the Pelicans a chance to pull themselves together.

There was no way for Andy to know what Ding had told them, but when the Pelicans went back into the game they seemed to have lost some of their excess zeal without sacrificing their determination. It added to their poise. Hagerty had sent in a replacement during the time-out period, with instructions to change into a six-man line. A passing team could be dangerous in this spot on the gridiron, and another defender in the backfield was essential for good pass defense.

Garson, aware of the new defensive setup, outsmarted himself a little. Seeing that the Pelicans were loosening their line-backers for a possible pass, Garson faked a quick pass to his right end, then sent Tragg on a delayed buck off tackle. Tragg, though he went in like a bullet, was slowed down at the line of scrimmage. He struggled a short distance into the Pelican backfield before he was brought down for a two-yard gain. The Pelicans had looked good on that one. The superior weight of their forward wall had at last paid off.

The Gulls' next play followed the same opening pattern of the one before, as if Garson figured he might catch the Pelicans off guard by repeating the same play. This time, however, he went to the air. He snapped a short pass to his right end, Stu Dover, who cut fast into the Pelican backfield.

The play was well planned, but Garson's pass was far from perfect. The average end could not have fielded it. Dover, however, offered quick proof that all the glowing reports about him must be true. The best he could do after a lunge and a long reach was to check the ball's flight with his left hand. The long fingers of his other hand clamped solidly about the ball as it came down. He regained balance with a few cat-like steps, but the Pelicans hemmed him in before he could squirm into the clear. The play, designed for a short gain, was successful. The referee called out the chain. It was a first down—by an inch or so. A discontented rumble traveled through the Pelican rooting section.

Andy shot a quick look at his father sitting regally among his retinue. Jocko was talking with some vehemence to the man beside him, but Andy did not doubt that Jocko's words were intentionally loud, intended for the audience about him. It was also reasonable to assume that his parent was expounding on the fact that a well-coached team would have long since stopped the Gulls. Andy's lips were tight when he returned his attention to the game.

The Pelicans had now been pushed into their own territory on the forty-seven-yard line. They were in trouble and they knew it. They smothered a couple of end sweeps with a defense which substituted violence for co-ordination. They squandered energy instead of hitting with the smooth precision they had learned from Hagerty. They succeeded, though, in holding the Gulls to five yards on the first two downs.

The Gulls passed on the third down. The Pelicans, anticipating a pass, red-dogged the passer. A pair of linemen crashed into the Gull backfield with a snarling eagerness that fouled their timing. Garson dodged them handily and got the pass away, whipping a sizzler toward Dover near the side line. The pass was on the beam.

Ding Kibby got across to cover. It looked to Andy as if the ball, Ding, and Dover all arrived at the same spot at the same time. It also looked to Andy as if Ding had made an honest effort to play the ball when he barged into Dover and broke up the pass. The umpire, however, saw it in a different way. It was, admittedly, a tough decision which might have gone either way, but the umpire gave the nod to Dover. He called pass interference, and the ball was retained by the Gulls, first down on the Pelican seventeen-yard line.

It was a rough decision for the Pelicans, a heartbreaker, the sort of thing to make a team begin to wonder if it might be jinxed. The Gulls did not permit the Pelicans much time for wonder. They scrambled from the huddle with the air of men who had to force their luck while it was riding high.

They faced a team of angry, desperate men. The Pelicans, though in the shadow of their own goal posts, had a tactical advantage. Their defensive area had been tightened. The line-backers would not have to cover so much ground. The Gulls were now in territory where the going was the toughest.

A line play lost a yard against the frantic, clawing Pelican defense. Garson tried another side-line pass, but had to hurry it when his protection failed to hold. He overshot his mark. He went for broke on the third down. He almost connected with Stu Dover in the end zone—not quite. Another end-zone pass was frighteningly close, but the ball went over to the Pelicans on downs.

Andy was sharply aware of the Pelican fans' reaction to their team's successful stand. There were only a few sincere yells of congratulation, and none of the noisy flood of relief which normally could be expected. The attitude appeared to be, "They should have stopped 'em sooner. We'll save our yelling till the Pelicans deserve it. Let's see what happens."

Andy could feel the waiting, watchful silence like a weight upon his back. It was unnatural, almost sinister, for a college football crowd to act like this. He also knew, with a tightening of his throat, that no group of fans *could* act like this unless the groundwork had been laid ahead of time, unless some outside force had worked its way into impressionable minds like termites gnawing on the rafters of a house.

The Gull rooters, by contrast, were demonstrating how a bunch of normal fans should act. They had gamely swallowed their disappointment that the Gulls had failed to score. They were making noise again, a lot of it, the sort of noise that sweating football players like to hear. It spoke of loyalty and confidence. The cheering packed a wallop.

While the ball was being brought out to the twenty-yard line, Andy was certain that the Pelicans were aware of the contrast between cheering sections. He saw them shooting glances toward their fans, puzzled glances, angry glances. They sensed, undoubtedly, the challenge being tossed at them— "Let's see you go to work! Show us something! Now's your chance. You've got the ball."

The rooters drove the message home. Andy saw it hit the mark. The Pelicans, it was reasonable to believe, would react in different ways, each man according to his temperament. It was also reasonable for Andy to assume that these reactions might go far toward messing up co-ordination, particularly if each man felt that the burden of proof rested upon him alone. No man could solve the present problem by himself, not without co-operation from the others, and such co-operation would depend upon eleven brains whose thoughts were closely meshed. When the Pelicans went into their huddle, Andy wiped the chilly moisture from his palms.

CHAPTER

13

WHEN the Pelicans bent forward in the huddle, Andy watched their backs. He saw several of them twitch with eagerness as if the owners were forcing themselves to stay in the huddle until Ding Kibby called the signal. When the huddle broke, the Pelicans hurried to the line of scrimmage with a speed which brought them to a skidding stop. They came into a crouch, poised for the snap of the ball which would hair-trigger them to action.

The dramatic, all-important moment fizzled out when a Pelican lineman jumped off side. Andy could see his teammates trying to retain their head of steam while the referee paced off the five-yard penalty. The huddle was repeated, then the quick burst to the line of scrimmage.

The Pelicans stayed on side this time. Their determination to avoid another penalty sliced a fraction of a second from their charge, making them vulnerable to the fast-hitting, lighter team. Ding had called for a

simple, off-tackle power play to test the strength of the
Gull line. The play might possibly have gained small
yardage had Mark Sutton been less eager to score a
touchdown on the opening play. As it was, Mark started
his charge before Ding had a chance to make an accurate hand-off. Ding did his best to correct the timing
error, but succeeded merely in jamming the ball against
Mark's hip instead of in his belly. Mark grabbed
frantically for the ball, and muffed it. Ding managed
to recover the fumble, beating a Gull lineman to the
ball by several inches. The bobble cost the Pelicans
three yards.

It was not a bright beginning for the Pelicans. It was,
in fact, a very sad performance, and their fans did not
let them forget it. Neither did the Gull fans. Andy saw
Ding call time out, an essential move to give the shaken
Pelicans a chance to pull themselves together.

Andy wondered bleakly if the men were equal to the
task. It was a rough one. Their high hopes and their
grim intentions had received a serious setback. It would
probably not have been serious in an ordinary game.
This, however, was not an ordinary game, and the men
would be inclined to magnify the matter beyond its
real importance. Andy understood the strain the Pelicans were under, a strain they had imposed upon themselves against Coach Hagerty's advice.

The Pelicans, as individuals, were definitely at fault.
In their present state of mind, unfortunately, they
would not recognize this fact. They were faced with the
huge task of reorganizing their thoughts in the brief,

two-minute time-out period. Andy hoped they would succeed.

There was small evidence of immediate success. Ralph Hopper, the fullback, carried the ball for three yards on a cross buck, merely gaining back the yards lost on the fumble. With the ball on the fifteen-yard line, third down, Ding sent Mark on a wide sweep around right end. Mark scrambled through for another four yards behind interference which could have been a whole lot better. The Pelicans kicked on the fourth down.

The game settled down to a pattern, not an encouraging pattern for the Pelicans. Their advantage in weight, together with their potentially better talent staved off disaster for a while. These advantages, on the other hand, were not enough to carry the ball across the Gull goal line. The Pelicans had several chances, all of which went down the drain through overeagerness or discouragingly bad breaks.

The Gulls, it is true, showed surprising strength. However, by all the laws of football, this strength should not have been enough to hold the Pelicans on even terms, as the Gulls unquestionably were doing, despite the fact that most of the good breaks fell in their direction. It was a toss-up game until the closing seconds of the second period. Then the lightning struck.

The Pelicans had the ball on the Gull sixteen-yard line, one of the Pelicans' best scoring chances of the day. With seconds left, Ding rightly figured that the Gulls would be expecting an end-zone pass. Instead,

Ding faked the long pass, then flipped a lateral toward Mark who had his interference out ahead of him.

Something, at this point, went horribly wrong. Archie Tragg, whether lucky or inspired, came out of nowhere. He snatched the short pass from Mark's very finger tips, and uncorked his formidable speed toward pay dirt.

Ding Kibby was alert enough to spot the threat while in the making. He was on the run before Tragg stole the ball. Both Ding and Tragg were in full stride with Ding a yard or so behind, almost, but not quite, close enough to make a tackle. Ding never got that close. He was fast, but not as fast as Tragg. Ding gave it everything he had, straining helplessly as the gap increased. Tragg was leading by five yards when he sailed across the goal line. The Gulls kicked the extra point. The score remained unchanged, 7-0, when the gun went off to end the half.

CHAPTER
14

ANDY did not anticipate the half-time session as he followed the Pelicans to the dressing room. He joined a bewildered, somber group of men. Some were frankly hangdog and ashamed. Others were inclined toward bluster, as if fearful they might be accused of treachery. Several seethed with outrage at the humiliation they had suffered. It formed a combination of emotions which did not tend toward solving the unhappy situation. The men looked apprehensively at Hagerty, expecting the blast they felt that they deserved.

Hagerty said, "Thanks for trying." There was no sarcasm in the words, merely a touch of sadness. After a moment he went on, "I can only repeat what I've been drilling into you for the past two weeks—don't try so hard. I don't have to tell you what's been going on out there, because you already know. Each one of you has been trying to lick the Gulls all by himself instead of helping the other guy or accepting help from him. I can only advise you. I can't play the game for you."

He let the words sink in before saying, "I'm forced to make one major change for the second half. I've got to have a man in there who can run down Tragg in case they shake him loose again. I think Jerry Holt might have that chance. I'm sorry, Ding."

Ding Kibby nodded. "Tragg's fast," he conceded, "but I think Jerry's faster. Tragg outran me."

Turning to Mark Sutton, Hagerty said, "I'm starting Joe Jasper at right half in the third period. It's no criticism of you, Mark, I've merely got to experiment with different combinations."

An angry flush came swiftly to Mark's face. He opened his mouth, but had sense enough to close it before the words came out. Hagerty spent the remainder of the rest period discussing technicalities of the Gulls' offensive and defensive game in an effort to relieve the tension of his men. When they left the dressing room, Andy was not entirely convinced that the coach had succeeded. The Pelicans were preoccupied and grim, with the air of men determined to teach the upstart Gulls a lesson they would remember. Andy saw Hagerty shake his head ever so slightly. It was a gesture of helpless resignation.

Mike greeted Andy's return with an accusing glare which demanded, "Where have *you* been?"

Andy scratched Mike's head, and Mike forgave him grudgingly for his absence. Andy turned his attention to the game as the Pelicans spread out to receive the kickoff. He tried to spot some indication that the Pelicans were in a proper frame of mind to play the sort of football of which he knew them to be capable. He saw nothing to encourage him. He saw even less to encourage him when the play got under way.

The game took up where it had left off. The Gulls played sound, co-ordinated football, making the best of their limited resources. The Pelicans resumed their frantic, badly timed efforts to prove that they could swamp the Gulls with touchdowns. The third period ended with the Pelicans still trailing 7-0, and with the Pelican fans contributing little more than sullen silence.

The unexpected happened when the teams were changing goals. Andy's breath jammed in his throat when Hagerty called, "Baker!"

Andy bounced to his feet as if someone had given him a hotfoot. He stared at the coach, and asked inanely, "Me?"

"Come here," said Hagerty, who was standing near the side line.

Andy reached his side in a couple of jumps. "Take over for Jasper," ordered Hagerty. Then, as if he felt Andy needed some sort of explanation, he added, "You and Jerry have always worked well together. On the double!"

Andy sprinted on the field, buckling his helmet as he ran, and feeling horribly conspicuous, a feeling which was suddenly exaggerated to a stage which made him slightly numb. His appearance on the field had stilled what little noise the Pelican fans were still inclined to make, and through the silence boomed a voice which had been trained to make each word distinct.

"Let's go, Andy boy! Let's go!"

Andy recognized the voice. He should have recognized it. It came from his proud parent, Jocko Baker, who, with the instinct of a trouper, had decided that the moment needed a touch of drama. It was also a fine chance for Jocko to project his famous voice, also to let the world know that he was loyal to his son. Jocko could hardly have been expected to pass up such a chance.

The words hit Andy in the back. They almost made him stumble. It was just the sort of inspiration, he reflected grimly, that he needed—needed as much as he needed a broken leg. He had almost forgotten Jocko's presence, a desirable condition that his father had eliminated. He was now reminded that his father would be watching every move in a demanding way. He was reminding Andy of this great opportunity to bring glory to the proud name of Baker.

"Oh, no!" groaned Andy, as he ran.

There was another angle, too, which worked its way maliciously into Andy's thoughts. There was bound to be speculation among certain of the fans that Andy was getting this big chance because his father had put on the pressure. Andy knew this was not true. Or *did* he know it?

He was certain of one thing, however, namely that his father's big send-off was not the thing he needed for his debut in varsity football. He was in no frame of mind to keep his thoughts upon the game, not, at least, until he had a chance to settle down a bit. He clung to the desperate hope that if he could pull himself together, he could prove he belonged in big-time football.

When he joined the squad Sam greeted him with pleased satisfaction. The other men were noncommittal with the air of, "We've tried everything else, we might as well try Baker. Things couldn't get any worse." Jerry Holt eyed Andy critically, probably sensing his agitation and making a mental note to use him sparingly until Andy got the feel of things.

The Pelicans had the ball on their own thirty-two-yard line, second down, four yards to go. In the huddle Jerry called for a fake by Andy on an off-tackle slant, assuming, logically enough, that the Gulls would be keeping a close eye on any new replacement, who might have been sent in to pull something tricky out of the bag or to display a special skill, whatever it might be.

It turned out to be a good guess on Jerry's part. His ball handling was deceptive despite poor co-operation from Andy, who got off to a jerky start. Jerry, however, managed to make the fake belly pass convincing enough to pull the Gull line-backers out of position when they moved over to stop Andy. Jerry completed his half spin and handed off to Ralph Hopper, who bucked the opposite side of the line for five yards and a first down.

Andy was piled up hard, but he liked the feel of it. It brought his attention back to football and the problems it presented. He was beginning to believe, in a cautious sort of way, that he might be of some help to the Pelicans. He went into the next huddle full of eagerness to prove it.

Jerry called for an option play on the first down, a short running pass if he could find a receiver. If he could not find one, he would run with the ball himself. Andy's job was to get out in front of Jerry, a job which Andy hurried to fulfill. He hurried so fast he left his spot before the ball was snapped. The referee slapped a backfield-in-motion penalty against the Pelicans and set them back five yards.

Andy waited in a state of shock for the wrath of the Pelicans to descend on him, but no great show of anger came in his direction. The Pelicans were willing to excuse him with resigned shrugs. This sort of thing had been going on all afternoon, and scarcely a man on the team had not been guilty of a similar infraction brought on by nerves and overeagerness. The Pelicans had suffered heavily through penalties. They were used to it.

The Pelicans, failing to regain the lost ground, were forced to kick, and the game returned to its previous seesaw battle. Andy had hoped that once involved in actual play, he would get the feel of things, and that his game would show its real potential. He got the feel of things, all right, and the feeling was not good.

It was all about him. It came from his teammates like a poisonous infection with no remedy available to cure it. Andy fought against it doggedly without success. It crept into his veins, and he was forced to share it with the others—the frightening necessity to accomplish something superhuman.

The Pelicans undoubtedly had tried and were still trying to heed Hagerty's advice, to play hard football and to think of nothing but the game of football, and very obviously they had failed. They had allowed their minds to be confused with something they considered more important than the game itself, an obligation to their coach to run up an imposing score. They had pushed themselves too hard. They had tried to substitute a berserk frenzy for co-ordination and team play.

Another thing struck Andy with a force which made the hunch seem valid. The Pelican fans were almost as guilty as the Pelicans themselves. It was something which Andy had not sensed while sitting on the bench. It was a whole lot different out here on the field.

In the past he had casually accepted the axiom that loyal fans can add strength to a team by loud, sincere support, but never, until now, had he understood the actual power a cheering section could exert. The Pelicans, today, were fighting themselves as well as their unresponsive fans. Andy could not close his mind against the sourness and the disapproval from the stands, and he knew that the effect of this was being felt by every member of the team.

To make things worse, the Pelicans were tired. They had squandered needless energy. There was no way to call it back, and the Gulls seemed well aware of this as the seconds of the fourth quarter clicked away. Their seven-point lead loomed larger all the time, and the game had reached the stage where the Gulls looked fairly safe in the game they had adopted—tight defensive football. They knew the Pelicans would be forced to open up with forward passes, a move which would increase the Gulls' chances to intercept a pass.

Andy was well aware that his own contribution to the Pelican cause was not spectacular. He made a few respectable gains while carrying the ball, but for the most part he was not impressive. The Pelicans, he realized, could have opened bigger holes for him. On the other hand he was fair enough to concede that his own timing was also at fault. Something was out of gear, yet he refused to blame anyone but himself.

He had to consider the possibility that the presence of his father was having some effect on him. He tried hard to forget about his dad, but subconsciously he knew he was trying to impress him. He was reasonably sure he was making as good a showing as Mark Sutton or Joe Jasper had made before him, no better and no worse. It was small consolation.

Disaster almost struck the Pelicans again when the Gulls, deep in their own territory, shook Tragg loose again. He might have traveled all the way except for Hagerty's foresight of putting Jerry Holt into the game. Jerry, with a handicap of several yards, uncorked a speed which should have left a contrail. He overhauled Tragg at mid-field and pulled him down. The

Pelicans then halted a conservative Gull attack to take possession of the ball again with a scant four minutes left to go.

They put the ball in play on their twenty-eight-yard line. It was a situation where running plays, even though effective, were unlikely to cover enough ground in time to beat the clock. The attack had to take place through the air. The Pelicans all knew it and, unfortunately, the Gulls knew it too. They could set their defense accordingly.

Jerry called a pass on the first down. Andy, as a possible receiver, enjoyed one of his few bright spots of the afternoon. He got off to a fast start when the ball was snapped. He sprinted into the Gull backfield, and when pass defenders closed in on him he cut suddenly toward the side line, heading toward the spot where Jerry would pinpoint the pass in the event he chose Andy as the receiver.

Andy's quick maneuver gained a few yards for him on the defenders. He turned at the right spot and saw the football coming at him. Everything had clicked on this play with a precision which seemed almost accidental in view of the poor timing of most previous plays. Everything depended now on Andy. His heart jammed in his throat, because he knew that no one but a butterfingered duffer could fail to catch a perfect pass like this.

He caught it! He pulled it in and hugged it tight. A quick glance showed him he would be cut off from an important gain, so he promptly stepped out of bounds to stop the clock and save some precious time. The gain was good for eighteen yards to bring the ball out to the forty-six-yard line.

A delayed impression became clear in Andy's mind as he started for the huddle. It occurred to him, with some surprise, that the successful pass had not been due entirely to a good performance by the Pelicans. The Gulls were tired. Their coach had juggled his undermanned team with considerable skill, but those still available for duty had definitely lost their steam.

The weakness became glaringly apparent on the next play. Jerry called for another pass, and when the ball was snapped, the Gulls fanned out to cover every possible receiver. They did an airtight job of it, but failed to cover Jerry. He stood for a moment, ball poised for the throw, and soon began to look a little silly and a little lonesome. He finally did the only thing left for him to do. He began to run.

Andy saw Jerry's change of play. Andy's pass defender saw it at the same time, but Andy managed to move a little faster than the other. When the Gull made a jerky move toward the ball carrier, Andy managed to throw an off-balance block, which, though clumsy, took the Gull out of the play. Andy bounced up to give Jerry further help if necessary, only to find that Jerry was doing all right by himself. He uncorked his blazing speed straight down the middle of the field, and not a single, weary Gull could lay a hand on him. He crossed the goal line standing up.

The Pelican fans acknowledged the touchdown in a

manner far from satisfactory. What noise they made had an undertone of, "It's about time. What held you up?" The Pelicans themselves showed grim relief, but no elation.

Trailing by one point, the Pelicans had no choice but to try for a two-point conversion. Hagerty sent the play in with a substitute. It was a sound play, well chosen, a power play through the line against the sagging Gulls. Ralph Hopper plunged across the goal line. Simultaneously the head linesman threw his flag upon the ground. The Pelican left tackle had been caught off side, a five-yard penalty. With the ball on the seven-yard line Jerry tried an end-zone pass. An alert Gull knocked it down. The score was still 7-6 in favor of the Gulls. There was a minute and forty-five seconds left to play.

A sizable number of Pelican fans began filing from the bleachers in disgust, unwilling to watch the final moments of the game. It was a deliberate slap in the face to the Pelicans, a pointed refusal to be associated with a team which could not even lick the Gulls. The Pelicans watched the exodus grim-faced. They got the message. They would have been stupid had they failed to get it.

They were gloomy and disheartened as they lined up for the kickoff. They had been beaten, and they knew it. The Gulls, with the ball in their possession, could easily run out the clock. They could cement their victory—a thundering upset.

Ralph Hopper's toe slammed angrily into the ball.

It was a fine kick whether it meant anything or not, but in this instance it turned out to mean a lot. It tumbled from the air down to the five-yard line. It came to the one person for whom it was not intended, Archie Tragg. And Tragg muffed it!

In the frantic scramble to retrieve the fumble, the Gulls' fatigue in mind and body became apparent at its worst. A careless foot nudged the ball into the end zone. There was another scramble to get the ball back on the field, and the Pelicans, quickly aware of the unexpected break, turned on their remaining speed.

Andy happened to be in the right spot at the right time. He arrived just as Archie Tragg got his hands on the ball. Tragg had no chance to straighten up and run. He was motionless, off balance. It was an easy tackle. Andy nailed him in the end zone for a two-point safety.

CHAPTER

15

It went down in the record books that the Pelicans of Gulf University had defeated the Gulls of Palmetto College in the opening game of the season by a score of 8-7. Among other impersonal statistics there was no mention of the callous performance of the Pelican fans who watched in silence as their victorious team went off the field.

There was no pride of accomplishment in the Pelicans themselves. They had set out to do a specific job, and they had bungled it. They could salvage but meager satisfaction from the fact that they had won, because they knew the one-point margin was undeserved. The Gulls had licked themselves. The Pelicans, in the dressing room, behaved like a defeated team.

"I feel as if I'd just come from a funeral," Andy said as he and Sam were walking home.

"Sort of gruesome, wasn't it?" conceded Sam.

"So where do we go from here?" asked Andy gloomily.

There was a forced determination in Sam's answer. "Where can we go but up? We can't get any worse than we were today."

"The thing that bugs me," Andy said, "is that *we* fouled it up, yet Hagerty will get the blame."

Sam nodded. "The stage has been all set for it."

Andy winced. Sam hastened to apologize, "I didn't mean that quite the way it sounded."

"What's the difference?" Andy shrugged. "I might as well get used to it. By this time everybody knows who set the stage. I only hope he won't blow things wide open right away."

Jocko played it cagey, although Andy could make a fairly accurate guess at his strategy. Jocko would continue working toward his goal—a new, high-powered coach for the Pelicans, because, once committed, Jocko was not the sort of person to back down. On the other hand, Andy believed that he had recognized a patient cunning in his parent which could control the impulse to get what he wanted when he wanted it.

In the present instance Jocko had, unquestionably, won his first important skirmish. The Pelicans had made a spectacle of themselves against the Gulls, a debacle for which the coach could easily be blamed. It could be assumed that any good coach would make the best of his material, and that no coach should use the alibi of claiming he could not control the mental attitude of his men.

Jocko appeared content now to let the pot simmer for a while, counting on the erratic emotions of an average student body to keep the flame alive beneath the pot. The seed of discontent had been expertly planted in fertile ground. It should flourish now with a minimum of nourishment, and when it had matured Jocko's purpose would be served.

If Jocko jumped in at the present moment with a loud, "I told you so! Now let's have a little action!" he would run the risk of being pegged as an impatient loud mouth. If he waited until the student body worked itself into a righteous lather he could then step on stage in the role of benefactor. He could announce, "Yes, kids, I agree with you. It's an awful mess. So you need a little help? Okay, kids, you can count on Uncle Jocko. I'll see that you get the sort of football team you deserve."

The student body simmered quietly, with no immediate threat of an explosion. Judd Hagerty ignored his men's hangdog, apologetic air as he set about the job of preparing the team for its rough schedule. He was dealing with a worried bunch of men who were trying hard to forget the humiliation of their opening game, who were trying, once again with too much urgency, to prove they were as good as they believed they were.

In the second game the Pelicans tangled with the Rebels, a strong team from Alabama. In this game it was no advantage to the Pelicans to be playing on their own field. The fans, at first, seemed tentatively willing to forgive, an attitude which faded when the Rebels scored a pair of touchdowns in the first period. The touchdowns, even though they were the result of lucky breaks, did not change the scoreboard, 14-0.

The Pelicans refused to fold. They played good football, showing occasional flashes of their real potential. In the second period they rammed across a touchdown of their own, then scored a conversion to make it 14-7.

Andy played for a short time in the final period. He had no chance to make a hero of himself, but was in there long enough to get the feel of things. It was better than the feeling in the Gull game, but it still lacked a lot. The men kept shooting irritated glances at the lukewarm fans. The Rebels scored again with a long run in the closing minutes of the game. The final score was 20-7.

Sam and Andy were back in Andy's room when Andy burst out, "I may be looking for an alibi, but those fans acted like a bunch of jerks! They didn't give us any help. I'll bet they robbed us of at least one touchdown, maybe two. Does that sound crazy?"

"It might have sounded crazy before the season started," Sam said thoughtfully, "but it doesn't sound so crazy now. I never realized before these last two games of ours how much a crowd could do for you. Of course, I've only played in front of high-school crowds, but I guarantee you, pal, that the right kind of yells can put a lot of stiffness in your spine. I missed it out there today. I could feel the difference. No, it doesn't sound so crazy now."

"But why," demanded Andy, puzzled, "can't we **go**

out there and play our best game of football just because we want to? Do we have to be prodded into it?"

"I'm no psychiatrist," said Sam, "but it looks as if we *do* have to be prodded into it. On a team of eleven men each man can't play just the way he wants to or think the way he wants to. He's got to play and think like the other ten, and to make this happen there's got to be a common incentive."

"We all want to win," Andy pointed out. "Why shouldn't that be enough?"

"I don't know," admitted Sam, "but apparently it's not enough to get the best results. Take the pros, for instance. Those guys play for dough. They're out to make a living, which is a mighty big incentive these days. But even they don't do their best without the support of their fans."

"I'll buy that," said Andy.

"Okay," said Sam, warming to his theme. "Now take college players like us. About the only common incentive we've got is the thing called school spirit. They pump us full of it, and most of the time it works. It's bound to bog down, though, if they don't keep pumping. Why should we want to fight and die for the dear old school without any encouragement from the school itself? And the fans represent the school. They're the ones that can hold a team together or shake it apart. If the fans are loyal to a team, it won't take the boys long to find it out, and if they know that the fans are behind them all the way, they can keep their minds on football and play a better game. Have I made any sense?"

"Yes. It makes the outlook for the rest of the season look pretty grim."

Sam nodded gloomily. "I'm afraid it does."

The fear was justified. The Pelicans improved some, but not enough to win the ones that counted. It was significant that their play was better in the games away from home. Unhampered by the criticism of their fans, they showed flashes of real football. Their handicap in these games came from an involuntary comparison of the host fans with their own. The difference was upsetting. The rival team got all the help it needed from the cheering section.

Andy got a chance to play in almost every game. The experiences were frustrating, because he, also, showed flashes of real football, just enough of them to make him keep on hoping that his game might someday be impressive if conditions ever changed. He had the baffling conviction that whatever football talent he had was being cramped, and he was willing to blame himself to some extent for this. He could not throw off the violent need to prove himself, to gain a prominence other than the one he now possessed, one which he alone could claim. It was a distracting urge which did not help his football.

Mark Sutton may have sensed this. He had made a poor job of hiding his resentment at the times Andy had been sent in as his substitute, but he had carefully avoided any open row with Andy, anything which might have lowered Mark's stock with Hagerty. Mark went about it in a different way. He slyly fostered the idea about the campus that Andy got a chance to play because his influential dad had wanted it that way. This news leaked through to Andy from a source he had to believe reliable.

Andy shouldered the new load with an angry resignation that he tried to keep from getting out of hand. He was more or less successful, but had to give the credit to his weekly jaunts with Sam in the *Tern*. The lazy underwater dives served as a strong antidote to their raveled nerves, and Mike the pelican, guided by some strange instinct, was always there to add a touch of comedy. Andy often invited members of the team as passengers, placing only one restriction on them—no football talk. Hagerty approved of the idea.

The football situation at Gulf University did not improve. It got a little worse, but not as bad as Andy and a lot of others had expected. A portion of the student body gradually adopted a lethargic attitude, an unstudied indifference to the football team which, in its way, was worse than open rebellion. These previous fans did not bother to attend the games.

The picture would not have been complete without the rival factions, those of strong opinions pro and con. It was inevitable that a core of loyal fans still manned their guns. Opposed to these were those convinced that Hagerty must go. It was hard to say which faction was the strongest, but the difference of opinion kept them bickering among themselves. The anti-Hagertys released their energy this way instead of in more violent demonstrations.

CHAPTER
16

THE Pelicans moved toward the end of another disastrous season, with little hope of salvaging much self-respect or much approval from their fans. The undercurrents on the campus were disruptive to the team and to the student body.

One day Sam Tedder and Andy were discussing the attitude of the alumni.

"It's been an eye opener to me," Sam summed it up. "You hear about it and you read about it, but until you've been right under the guns you'd never believe how much harm a bunch of meddling old grads can do a school. They've almost ruined this one. They want what *they* want, not what the school wants or what is good for it. They've done a good job here at Gulf. They've stirred things up until they'll probably get what they're after—a new coach. It makes me sick."

"Me too," concurred Andy. Then, after a short silence, "I wonder if we're not partly to blame, the football men, I mean."

"The football men?" Sam exclaimed indignantly. "Are you nuts? We've knocked our brains out trying to carry the load the old grads have dumped on us."

"We've knocked our brains out in the games," conceded Andy, "but it just struck me that we may have been sort of dumb in other ways."

"How?" Sam challenged.

"Well," said Andy, lining up his thoughts, "we know there's a strong underground working against Hagerty in the school. Has it ever occurred to us to start a strong underground of our own?"

"Keep talking," Sam invited, showing interest.

"We've played the best football we know how, and for the most part have let it go at that. Why don't we wise up and start a campaign of our own, starting at the grass roots to convince some of our half-witted fans that the old grads are playing them for suckers, making chumps of them?"

"It might work," said Sam excitedly. "It's late to start, but it just might work."

"It should help, at any rate," said Andy. "You can't shrug off the fact that football men are important on any campus, and they swing some weight. Up to now, all we've been doing is griping over a bad deal, but if our boys start doing a little hard missionary work, we may convince the students in this school that they're the ones who are getting the bad deal."

"Where do we start?"

"We're first-year men on the team," Andy pointed out. "We'll plant the thought with some of the old-timers like Ding Kibby, because their opinions will carry a lot more weight than ours. If they like the idea they can start working on it."

The Pelicans liked the idea fine. They were, for the most part, annoyed with themselves for not having taken countermeasures sooner. Ralph Hopper summed it up, "We've been all muscles and no brains. We've let the old grads bang us around like tackling dummies. It's mighty late for us to start planting our own propaganda, that's for sure. But what have we got to lose?"

The campaign got under way as the Pelicans tried to make up for lost time. Andy was not foolish enough to expect spectacular results during the brief remainder of the season. He was pleasantly surprised to find that the Pelicans' efforts were even partially successful in the face of the alarming prospect of the last two games.

They were conceded no chance at all against the Texas Rams, a team which had weathered a rough schedule with but a single loss. The final game promised to be even worse. The Pelicans would wind up their dismal season in the traditional game against the Miami Marlins, and the outlook was depressing. The Pelicans and the Marlins had waged annual, bruising battles for the past eighteen years. Both teams had had their ups and downs and the rivalry was bitter.

On the years when one team was stronger than the other, the stronger team did not let up for one malicious instant. It kept pounding away with everything it had, delighted to make the score humiliating and lopsided, and the Marlins were gleefully anticipating such a rout this year. They were loaded with a power which had kept them undefeated for the season. They were headed for the Orange Bowl with a confidence that had prompted them to issue tickets in advance. It merely remained for them to brush aside the feeble Pelicans, a pleasure which would be increased by meeting the Pelicans on their own field in front of their own fans.

During the week preceding the game against the Rams, Andy was almost certain that the student body's attitude toward the football team was undergoing a change. There seemed to be a growing element of doubt among the fans, as if they were weighing the possibility that their judgment of Coach Hagerty might have been a little hasty.

Andy took no part in the campaign. The regular members of the team spread the propaganda, and their word, he was assured, would carry considerably more weight than his. There were moments, though, when he began to doubt this line of reasoning, causing him to wonder if he was deliberately avoiding something which, involving his own father, might turn out to be unpleasant. He was beginning to wonder if he actually lacked guts to assert himself, a matter which came to an unexpected head through no instigation of his own.

Andy and Sam returned to the dormitory after a late meal at the training table. They found a heated argument in progress at one end of the lounge. A group of a half-dozen men were wrangling over the most potent issue on the campus.

Dispelling any doubt as to the subject of the argument, a loud voice said, "He's had his day. Hagerty may be a nice guy and all of that, but what this school wants is a good football team."

Sam stopped in his tracks. Andy, taking another hopeful step toward the elevator, found himself trapped in a situation which left him little choice of action. When Sam started slowly toward the group, Andy fell in step behind him.

Andy was surprised and somewhat puzzled at the type of men involved in the debate. He knew them all, and none was the sort of man who would deliberately stir up trouble just to pass the time. They were all good students, conscientious guys. The man, in fact, who was demanding Hagerty's scalp was Ray Conlin, a senior and a respected member of the Student Council. It was rather frightening to Andy that men of Conlin's caliber should take a stand against Coach Hagerty.

"Hi, Ray," Sam greeted casually. "You got troubles?"

Conlin said, "Hi, Sam, hi, Andy," without enthusiasm. Then, testily, "Have *we* got troubles? You're the ones who've got the troubles—you football chumps who get your brains knocked out while Hagerty calls the shots."

Sam grinned, conceding, "Our brains get shaken up a bit, that's for sure, but don't you think we might have just a few left?"

"Don't make me say it," Conlin growled.

"I'm not kidding," Sam persisted mildly. "Give me

a straight answer, Ray. Do you honestly believe we're stupid?"

Conlin shifted uneasily in his chair before saying irritably, "Of course I don't think you're stupid. So where do we go from here?"

"It's a simple, logical progression," Sam continued. "We're the ones who take the beating. Why do we keep taking it? Wouldn't we be the first to know if Hagerty was a lousy coach? Wouldn't we be the first ones to climb on the band wagon if we didn't think he was the best coach in the league?"

"What are you getting at?" demanded Conlin cautiously. "If we've got a good coach, why don't we win games? Do we lack good material?"

"The material's good, the fans are bad," Sam stated flatly.

"Oh, come on now!" exploded Conlin. "What sort of an alibi is that?"

"Did you ever play football or any spectator sport?"

"No."

"Then you don't know what a loyal bunch of fans can do for you. You don't know what it's like to try to give the best you've got while the fans give you the glassy eye. The Pelicans are willing to give the best they've got. So what about you and a lot of others like you? Has it ever occurred to you to get behind your team instead of sabotaging it? Has it ever occurred to you that a few old grads are leading you around by the nose?"

An angry reflex brought Conlin halfway from his

chair. Sam's big hand pushed him gently back. Conlin glared at Sam for a moment then transferred his glare to the ceiling of the lounge. Sam finally broke the heavy silence.

"Well?"

Ray Conlin let his breath out slowly, swallowed hard and said, "You're right, of course. It's hard for me to say so, Sam, but it looks as if I've been the chump. I've switched sides as of now." He forced a rueful grin, then asked suddenly, "Where do you fit into the picture, Andy?"

It was a pointed, loaded question. Conlin was the sort of man who, even when he changed his mind, preferred to keep the record clear. He caught Andy by surprise. The startled look in Andy's eyes confirmed it. The eyes of the other men were fastened on him now, and he faced the showdown with an odd sense of relief.

He demanded bluntly, "You're asking if I'm backing Hagerty or Jocko Baker?"

Conlin nodded. "That's the size of it."

"I'm backing Hagerty. I think my father's wrong— dead wrong, and from now on I'm going to have the guts to say so."

There was no more tension in the group. When Sam and Andy started for the elevator, Sam said, "We're making progress. It's probably much too late, but then —who knows?"

In confirmation of the fact that the Pelicans' campaign was having an effect, a larger crowd than was expected attended the Ram game. The Rams lived up to their advance notice. They were strong, rugged, and well-balanced. They did not, however, tear the Pelicans to shreds according to pre-game predictions. The Pelicans put up a battle. There were short periods when they were truly formidable, and Andy, wondering whether or not he had imagined it, seemed to feel that these periods came at times when the fans momentarily forgot their prejudice and let out honest yells of encouragement. The Rams came out on top, but the Pelicans were not disgraced by the final score of 20-14.

Despite the loss, there was a gentle undercurrent of excitement in the dressing room. The reason for it was not well enough defined for any of the Pelicans to put into words, they merely seemed to sense that something strange had happened to them out there on the field, an occasional feeling of strong unity, which might easily come to them again in greater force.

Before leaving the dressing room Andy invited several of the Pelicans for a boat ride on the following day. They accepted promptly, glad for the chance to rest their bruised bodies in the sun, and probably to get in a little fishing. The *Tern*'s passengers would be Ding Kibby, Jerry Holt, Ralph Hopper, and Joe Jasper. Andy and Sam would constitute the crew.

"Make it about ten-thirty," Andy said. "Don't worry about lunch. I'll have plenty of food on board."

Everyone showed up on time. Before they had a chance to leave, Mark Sutton with several of his friends came on the pier, having obviously planned an outing of their own on Mark's boat, the *Lone Star*. The greetings between Mark and the other Pelicans were perfunctory. Mark's teammates, though conceding his ability as a first-string halfback, were frankly cool toward him as a person. Mark chose to accept their attitude toward him as complimentary, an indication they were jealous of his prowess as a football star. It was a far-fetched type of reasoning, but it suited Mark.

"Where to?" asked Sam, as they headed into Tampa Bay.

"There's a good diving spot outside the keys off Sarasota," Andy said. "We're getting an early start, and can make it easily enough. It's not too deep there and the water's clear. There are some nice coral formations down there, and usually a lot of interesting fish."

"Suits me," said Sam.

"How about you guys?" Andy asked the rest.

"Who cares?" Ding answered for the group.

Mike arrived about that time. He soared above the *Tern,* approving its passenger list before favoring them with his presence. Everything seemed to check out all right, so he made a few preliminary circles to test the wind and the boat's speed before lowering his flaps.

His approach for a landing was always a matter of exciting speculation. He always appeared as if he would never make it, and today was no exception. Everyone forgot to breathe while Mike was coming in. He hit his target, flapped his wings for balance, and managed to stay put. As soon as he regained composure he acknowledged the applause. His scornful bearing seemed to say, "Ya-a-ah, fooled you that time."

An hour or so later, Sam said, "Looks like we're being tailed."

Andy reached for the binoculars and focused them astern. "It's the *Lone Star,*" he announced with some annoyance.

"Maybe he's just heading someplace that takes him in the same direction," Sam said optimistically.

"Don't count on it," warned Jerry. "He knows we're out here to enjoy ourselves, and he's just the sort to horn in where he knows he's not wanted. It's his idea of humor."

Andy was hoping for the best when they reached their destination and dropped anchor. The *Lone Star* was some distance away, and there was still the possibility that Mark was heading for a point farther down the coast. While the *Tern* rocked gently on the swells, Andy and Sam began to don their scuba gear. The others, wearing bathing trunks, soaked up the sun as they loafed on deck.

Mike, from his lookout position on the bow, began to get disturbed. He raised enough commotion to draw attention to himself. Ding Kibby was the first to spot the cause of Mike's agitation.

Ding leaped to his feet, pointed a rigid arm, and yelled, "Shark! Shark! Shark!"

Needless to say, he drew the attention of the others. An excited group of football players gazed at the awesome spectacle of a triangular fin slicing through the water. It was a satisfying thrill for those who had never seen the sight before.

Ralph Hopper said, "It could be just a porpoise." The others turned to Andy for confirmation.

"It's a shark, all right," said Andy.

"You're not going in the water with that thing, are you?" Ding demanded with concern.

"It's probably just a ground shark," Andy said. "You see them now and then in shallow water near the shore. They're considered harmless."

"You didn't answer my question," persisted Ding.

Andy grinned. "No, we won't go down till he clears out. The chances are he wouldn't be any more dangerous than a goldfish, but there's no sense in being stupid about it. I've never heard of a ground shark attacking anybody, but I suppose there could always be a first time under the right conditions. How about it, Sam?"

Sam nodded. They were taking off their air tanks when the *Lone Star* pulled alongside, reversed its motors, and stopped some twenty feet away. Mark saw Sam and Andy slipping out of their tank harness.

Mark called across, "What's the matter, boys? Water too cold for you today?"

Jerry broke the news. "We saw a shark."

Mark considered this. Andy could almost see the wheels working in his mind. Mark was checking off the things all skin divers are supposed to know about sharks.

"What kind was it, Andy? One of those big bad ground sharks?" Mark finally asked.

"That's probably what it was," said Andy.

"So you let it scare you off," jeered Mark. "You know they wouldn't hurt you."

"Maybe not."

Mark was enjoying himself. He sounded off again. "So you're chicken, huh?"

Andy held his temper. "Look, Mark," he said evenly, "if you don't like to associate with cowards, you've got the whole Gulf of Mexico behind you. There's lots of room out there."

Mark opened his mouth for a comeback, then closed it slowly. Andy watched an alarming thought bang home into Mark's mind, and he knew exactly what it was. Mark had outtalked himself and he had just begun to realize it. He had blurted irresponsible accusations, and in doing so he had boxed himself into a corner. If he accepted Andy's suggestion to shove off, he would tacitly admit that he, too, was scared to go into the water. He had loudmouthed himself into a jam with but a single exit. He would have to save face now, with his own pals and with the football players. The decision came hard, but he made it. There was forced bluster in his laugh.

"Will you take the chance if *I* go in first?" he demanded.

Andy turned his back, placing Mark more than ever on the spot. Andy hoped he would back out, but Mark had gone too far for that. He began to don his scuba gear with an air of grim determination rather than of willingness. Andy replaced his own tank on his back.

"Don't be a chump," protested Jerry. "You've taken enough stuff from that jerk. Let him play the hero if he wants to."

Andy shook his head. "He's in no shape to go down alone. He's nervous." Then, grinning, "So am I, but I've spent more time under water than he has."

Sam said, "I'll go along."

"Not this time," Andy told him. "It—well, it's sort of personal."

"I guess it is," Sam conceded worriedly. "Just the same, I'll keep my gear on."

Andy saw something on the other boat that caused him quick concern. Mark had armed himself with a spear gun, a rubber-powered arbalete.

"The crazy fool," said Andy. "He could get himself in trouble with that thing."

"Better warn him," Ding suggested.

"He wouldn't listen," Andy said.

Before inserting the mouthpiece, Mark called across, "Let's go, brave guy!"

There was an unnatural tightness in Mark's voice. Clutching the spear gun, he entered the water with a backdrop, a foolish practice for an amateur. Andy noted he had sense enough to hold the mask in place with his free hand. Andy used the boarding ladder to go in.

Once submerged, Andy was well aware that his own nerves were somewhat skittery, a condition which was partially balanced by his annoyance at Mark, who had pressured him into a ridiculous situation. Even though he was reasonably certain he had nothing to fear from the shark, he still hoped sincerely that the arrival of the *Lone Star* had frightened the beast into taking its business somewhere else.

He had no trouble finding Mark, who seemed very willing to be found and who appeared in no hurry to go anywhere. He had stopped to cock his spear gun. With his feet against the foot braces and the butt against his body, he pulled the heavy rubber bands back into the load position to transform the spear gun into an ugly, lethal weapon. When the gun was cocked, Mark continued his cautious paddling, turning his head frequently to look in all directions.

Mark was first to see the shark. The warning came to Andy through Mark's frozen, petrified position in the water. Following the direction of Mark's eyes, Andy saw the dim bulk of the underwater animal moving lazily in their direction. He also saw Mark jerk into frantic action as he lined the spear gun on its target.

Words formed in Andy's mind, "No! No! You idiot! Don't do it!"

The words, unfortunately, could not reach Mark. He touched the trigger and the spear whipped from its groove. Andy momentarily disobeyed an underwater rule. He forgot to breathe, knowing that a wounded shark of any species could be dangerous, and that the chances of a fatal shot were negligible at such long range. Then Andy's breath came back in a surge of vast relief when the shark, confirming it had not been hit, continued its slow progress toward the divers.

In a matter of seconds there was only one diver for the big fish to investigate. Mark gave way to panic and went thrashing toward the surface some thirty feet away, a stupid act that gave Andy another bad scare, because he knew that sharks, if inclined to attack, would be more apt to go for a retreating, active quarry.

Andy wedged this thought firmly in his mind. Even though the shark showed no particular interest in the fleeing Mark, Andy dared not take the risk that the beast would pass up a second chance. Andy, at the moment, did not even blame Mark for his frantic scramble toward the surface, because Andy himself felt the almost overpowering urge to do it too. He fought against his panic, calling on his common sense to keep his nerves from snapping.

It was not easy. He forced himself to recall what all skin divers are supposed to know, primarily that the terror usually associated with the very name of *shark* can easily be exaggerated. As this one came still closer, Andy was somewhat reassured by its stubby, broad appearance which, together with its rear dorsal fin, identified it as a ground shark.

Andy tried to remind himself that ground sharks are supposed to be harmless. This one did not look harmless. Allowing for the magnifying effect of water, he judged it to be about twelve feet in length—a big one. Andy carefully unsheathed his knife, even though he believed the gesture might be just a bit on the dramatic side.

The shark stopped ten feet away, wondering probably what strange breed of fish he had encountered. Andy sweated out the staring contest for about thirty seconds, which seemed more like thirty minutes. He then recalled a theory that most sharks, though eager to attack a fleeing object, back away from anything of comparable size that moves toward them, the idea being, in shark psychology, that anything rash enough to move to the attack must be really dangerous.

Andy tried it. It took all of his remaining courage, but he moved a foot or so toward the ugly hulk in front of him. The shark moved back an equal distance. Andy tried to put determination in his next advance. The shark retreated. Then with an air of, "Shucks, he doesn't look too appetizing anyway," he turned and swam away.

Andy, unashamed, took time to pull himself together. He had to make several attempts to resheath his knife, because his hand was shaking. He had not enjoyed his visit with the shark. This was his first close encounter, and he hoped fervently it would be his last. He was almost ready to start up when Sam came surging down, alarm in every movement. Andy made the okay sign. Sam nodded with relief and they started up together. The men aboard the *Tern* let out a yell when the two heads came to the surface. They climbed on deck to face excited questions.

"It was a ground shark," reported Andy. "He wasn't out for trouble, and if I sound brave and casual, forget it. I was scared to death."

"*You* were scared?" exploded Ding. "You should

have seen our hero Sutton when he reached the top. He tried to keep on going right up through the air. He was yelling as if the shark had him by the leg. He put on quite a show. When they got him in the boat he ducked into the cabin and we haven't seen him since."

Andy glanced toward the *Lone Star,* noting that Mark's friends were lifting the anchor with embarrassed haste. They got the *Lone Star* under way and headed home as if to spend as little time as possible with their host.

"He turned out to be a yellow slob," growled Ding. "He left you down there by yourself. How do we know he won't let us down in a football game?"

A strange feeling came over Andy. He resented it, particularly at this time, yet he was forced to put it into words. He said, "Look, fellows, don't get the idea I've got any love for Mark Sutton, but right now I'm honestly sorry for the guy."

"*What?*" demanded Jerry. "After the way he's tried to throw the harpoon into you?"

"This is different," said Andy doggedly. "I've had twenty times the underwater experience he's had, yet I was scared silly when I met that shark. If I'd been as new to diving as Mark Sutton, I can't say I wouldn't have acted the same as he did, and none of you can say you wouldn't have acted the same way either. Some funny things can happen to you down there."

"Okay, okay," said Ding impatiently. "So maybe any of us would have chickened out, too. The point is we all *saw* Mark do it, and it's going to be mighty hard to forget."

"It'll be hard for Mark to forget, too," Andy pointed out. "But the worst part is, how is it going to affect the team?"

Ding considered this, and shook his head. "Not good," he prophesied. "Not good."

CHAPTER

17

THE story about Mark Sutton and the shark traveled fast around the campus. When he reported for practice Monday afternoon, he encountered the strained reception he had obviously expected. He met it with more than his accustomed swagger, even though he was smart enough not to attempt his usual wisecracks. He might have improved the situation by a frank admission he had lost his nerve the day before, but Mark was not the type to make a confession of this sort.

Hagerty drove the Pelicans hard in preparation for the week-end game against the Marlins. He scrimmaged them against formations the Marlins were known to favor, and early in the scrimmage it was evident that things were going badly. It was not hard to trace the trouble to its source—Mark Sutton.

It was hard for Andy to determine exactly what was going on, except that most of the plays centering around Mark failed to click. Most of them just missed, it is true, but a near miss in football can foul up almost any play. When a backfield star is involved in these near misses the results can be disastrous.

It was not easy to pinpoint the blame. Had Andy wanted to play a guessing game, there were a variety of guesses. Mark might have been trying too hard to overcome the prejudice he knew existed. There was the chance, too, that the ordeal of the day before might have robbed Mark of his blustering confidence. The Pelicans also had to be considered. It was possible that their confidence in Mark had been too badly shaken, but whatever the cause, or combination of causes, the Pelicans were playing sloppy football.

They had every right to be discouraged as they faced these new and serious complications. They had every right to dread the thrashing they were bound to get when they tangled with the Marlins, yet the morale of the Pelicans, instead of sagging, showed improvement. It was not the final summoning of courage expected from a martyr, it was the real stuff, stemming from discovery that no situation is entirely hopeless.

The development was gradual. It started in the game against the Rams and continued its slow, experimental growth as if each side was cautiously testing the reaction of the other. The Pelicans continued their campaign against old-grad propaganda, and the fans appeared in greater numbers at the practice sessions. They came in a shamefaced sort of way, apologizing by their presence for their previous neglect.

Circumstances made the change a great deal more effective than it might otherwise have been. The fans were obviously not showing a fresh interest in their team because they felt the Pelicans had any chance at all against the Marlins. It was more in the nature of a slow awakening, as if they finally realized what the Pelicans had gone through this season, getting their brains knocked out in game after game without the slightest help from those most qualified to help—the fans.

The Pelicans began to play sharp, hard-hitting football when Hagerty was finally forced to take Mark Sutton from the line-up. If the Pelicans missed their most reliable ground gainer they made no mention of it. Joe Jasper moved into Mark's spot, and, even though he lacked Mark's natural ability, his greater experience was an asset. The Pelicans also showed a greater confidence in Joe than they had shown in Mark for the past few days.

There was virtually no build-up for the Marlin game, none of the hoopla that usually precedes a game between two bitter rivals, no boastful placards such as, *Hook the Marlins! We'll have fish for dinner!* The avoidance of these things was not a matter of maintaining dignity, it was just that the student body did not want to make a fool of itself by broadcasting a lot of vainglorious claims which, by no stretch of imagination, could be realized. They adopted an attitude of calm acceptance that the Pelicans would get licked, but that they, the fans, would not belly-ache about it this time. There was room for improvement in their attitude, but considerable belated progress had been made.

Andy had taken advantage of several opportunities

to contribute to this progress. On these occasions he had thrown his support wholeheartedly behind Coach Hagerty, letting it be known that he opposed his father on the issue of the coach. In doing this he built within himself a confusion of conflicting pride and guilt. He was proud to help the Pelicans as much as possible, yet he could not help but feel that he was pulling a quarterback sneak on his dad, a feeling which finally needled his conscience to the point of direct action.

Jocko Baker would have passed up a command performance at the White House before he would have missed a Pelican-Marlin game. He flew in on Friday afternoon, and Andy, after a light workout and a football movie session, found time to call on his father at the cottage. It was not the sort of call that Andy cared to make. It was something he just had to do. He came directly to the point as soon as he and Jocko were alone.

"I've got to get something off my chest," he said abruptly.

They were sitting in the patio. Jocko took time to relight his cigar and blow a smoke ring. "Fire away, son," he invited. "But don't expect me to act too surprised."

Andy thought this over before saying cautiously, "Then you must know what's been going on."

Jocko nodded. "I've got spies. The natives are getting restless."

"Did you know I've had a part in it?"

Jocko nodded again. "Yes. Good headline—son tries to knife father in the back."

Andy's lips went tight. Before he could think of anything to say, Jocko broke in hurriedly, "I didn't mean it that way. It was a gag and not a very good one." Andy relaxed a bit and Jocko went on, "I was sore at first. I'll admit it. When I had a chance to think it over, I also had to admit that you have as much right to your opinions as I have. The important thing to me, son, is that you're here to talk it over with me."

Andy let his breath out, and said, "Thanks." Then thoughtfully, "I'm sure we've been making headway with the student body, but I don't know how much. I *do* know that something funny has been going on around the campus for the past few days, but neither Sam nor I know what it is. No one will tell us—that is, of course, if there's anything to tell."

"Thanks for the tip, kid," Jocko chuckled. "But don't worry about your old man. He knows the angles. I'm sorry we're on different sides right now. Maybe it'll be different someday."

"I hope so," Andy said sincerely, as he rose to leave.

A surprisingly large crowd showed up for the traditional pre-game mass meeting in the stadium. Thousands of fans took seats in the bleachers. A wide platform had been constructed at the edge of the field on the fifty-yard line. It would seat the football squad and the dignitaries, prominent among whom would be that loyal alumnus, Jocko Baker. Jocko's presence, however, raised an uncomfortable doubt as to whether the crowd was on hand to honor the football team or to enjoy the free show Jocko had so generously promised them. For the last few years he had entertained them at this rally.

The Pelicans came directly to the stadium from a blackboard session with Coach Hagerty. Andy had a chance to exchange only a few perfunctory words with his father before the president of the university moved to the microphone to get things under way, explaining in the voice he used for jocularity, "We've got to hurry up and get our football boys to bed."

Andy, once he had settled in his chair, experienced the disturbing feeling that the crowd in front of him was acting strangely. It was definitely not a normal crowd, not the kind to be expected at a rally of this sort. There was an air of tension, something almost sinister as if it had been prearranged. It was a weird comparison, but Andy was reminded of a hungry cat waiting at a mouse hole.

He turned to Sam sitting at his side. "Do you feel it, Sam?"

Sam nodded. "Yes, and I don't like it. Maybe they're all waiting to give us the big raspberry."

"I hadn't thought of that."

Most of the other Pelicans must have held the same idea as Sam. They sat in their chairs as if braced against an unknown threat, and their eyes swept back and forth across the crowd. The other guests upon the platform displayed the same uneasiness. Jocko Baker was the only one who seemed completely unconcerned.

The president's voice was somewhat strained by the time he completed his opening address. He launched

hurriedly into the glowing introduction of "an illus-
trious alumnus who needs no introduction, Mr. Jocko
Baker." The president resumed his chair with an air
of relief, assured that the experienced Jocko could handle such a situation, and that his dynamic humor could
cope with the strange behavior of the fans and bring
them into the proper mood for the remainder of the
ceremony.

Jocko, equally assured, left his chair and approached
the microphone, his hands half-raised in a depreciating
gesture to acknowledge the expected burst of applause.
His hands sank slowly to his sides in a bewildered, flut-
tering sort of way. Andy felt a nasty chill along his
spine. The odd conduct of the fans was now explained.
They greeted Jocko Baker with a stony silence.

Jocko stood for a moment weathering the impact.
Andy could see his father's shoulders twitch as he
braced himself against the worst thing that can happen
to an entertainer. He tried a couple of experimental
gags in a voice not entirely steady. There was no re-
sponse. But Jocko would not quit. He went into one of
his most famous routines—a man trying to make an important call from a phone booth while holding a big,
active dog upon a leash.

Jocko gave it everything he had. It was a fine performance, one of Jocko's best. He went through the
entire routine from start to finish, unencouraged by a
single snicker from his audience, and at this point
Andy knew his dad was working on sheer guts. Andy
suffered with his father, scarcely knowing why except,

for the first time in his life, he was proud of Jocko Baker.

Jocko was perspiring freely by the time the act was over. He stood for a moment firmly erect, facing the devastating silence with the air of a man who was satisfied that he had done his best. Andy moved, then, scarcely aware that he had done so. He left his chair, drawn by an impulse he could not control. There was something stiff and trancelike in the walk that carried him beside his father. He stood there, wondering vaguely what had brought him.

Jocko said, "Thanks, kid." His voice was husky.

Andy touched his father's arm. It was a brief, involuntary gesture. Andy felt stiff muscles underneath his touch. The stiffness was no longer there when he removed his hand. Andy went back to his chair and sat down, still wondering why he had done the thing that he had done, yet glad that he had done it. He heard and saw a ripple of confusion travel through the fans. Jocko took advantage of the moment, speaking quietly into the microphone.

"You probably heard me thank my son. I am now sincerely glad of this opportunity to thank you."

The silence held while Jocko took a little time to choose his words. He seemed to have trouble finding them, an unusual situation for a man like Jocko Baker. He finally said, "Some people have to learn the hard way. I must be one of those. You've jammed the lesson home, kids, in a way that I can understand.

"I won't apologize for what I've done, because I

must have believed that I was doing right. Okay, I goofed." He paused, took a firm two-handed grip on the microphone, then spaced his next words carefully. "I'm through meddling in your affairs—and that's a promise. Don't count me out, however, if you ever need my help—and ask for it. That's all, kids."

The silence stirred convulsively as if a tight lid were resisting efforts to be pried off. It came off with an explosion, a concentrated roar that swept the speakers' platform like a gale. Andy saw his father step back slightly from its force, then stand in obvious confusion to accept the greatest ovation he had ever had, or probably ever would have.

Sam said with wonder in his voice, "He's quite a guy. You can be proud of him."

"I am," said Andy, blinking hard.

When the tumult had subsided somewhat, a voice yelled from the crowd, "Hey, Jocko! Do the phone booth act again!" So Jocko did the phone booth act again and laid 'em in the aisles.

When the rally was breaking up, Sam said, "I'll bet they tear the town apart tonight."

"I rather doubt it," Andy said.

He was watching the fans move from the stadium. Sam watched them too, before admitting, "Looks like I made a bad guess."

The fans were moving in a quiet way, not with the hopped-up enthusiasm of people heading for a celebration. They were behaving in a thoughtful manner, as if the occasion did not call for celebration, but rather for careful thought. They seemed to be weighing the significance of what had happened. Whooping it up at a time like this was just for kids, and many of these undergraduates had been introduced tonight to maturity.

Andy had a few words with his father before hurrying off to bed. Both of them were ill at ease, but Andy, with a feeling of quick warmth, knew that the way was open now for closer understanding. He found it easier than in the past to accept his father's invitation to a big steak dinner following the game.

Andy anticipated a restless night. He did not expect to sleep much, yet, once in bed, he found himself surprisingly relaxed. Thoughts of the game on the following day caused brief quivers of excitement which were counteracted by an unfamiliar peacefulness he had not known in weeks. He felt that something of great importance had been settled, or at least was on its way to being solved. He slept well and awoke refreshed.

The Marlin invasion took place in the morning. The fans arrived in cavalcades of buses and in private cars. Andy, at first, was puzzled that so many of the Marlin fans had bothered to make the long trip for what, to them, was a relatively unimportant game so far as league standing was concerned. He concluded that the rivalry between the two schools was greater than he had imagined. The Marlin rooters were not on hand to watch their boys win an easy game, they were on hand to see the Pelicans slaughtered. It was the sort of spectacle which would delight them.

When Andy reported for the game he entered the

dressing room with a strong feeling of curiosity, wondering how the outcome of the rally might have changed the Pelicans. He kept an open mind, not trying to guess whether they would be exuberant, savagely determined, or just plain apprehensive.

He was surprised to encounter none of these moods among his teammates. The Pelicans apparently were just as curious as Andy, glancing at one another for some cue as to how they should behave or think. They were all aware that they were facing some sort of sudden change, that they had been dropped without warning into an unfamiliar situation. There was no way for them to know what might await them when they reached the field. Whatever happened would depend greatly on their fans, and none of the Pelicans, by this time, considered himself an authority on fan reaction.

They were offered nothing definite when they went out for their preliminary warm-up. It was somewhat encouraging to see that the Pelican rooters were out in force. A great number of people other than students were also there. The stadium was jammed, a development, Andy reasoned, which might have stemmed from Jocko's spectacular part in the rally of the previous evening. Curiosity might have dragged a lot of people from their homes.

The fans were well-behaved and not too noisy. Most of the noise came from the Marlin side of the field, a continuous, derisive racket as they put the needle to their rival fans across the way. The Marlin fans, in a holiday mood, were having fun as they waited in happy anticipation for the massacre to start.

The Marlins themselves seemed to feel the same way about it. Their warm-up was in the nature of a playful, carefree romp. They had no worries. They were headed for the Orange Bowl, and that was that, but even in their casual warm-up they looked dangerous. They had weight and power and speed, together with another valuable ingredient—firm belief in their ability.

When the Pelicans came back to the dressing room for a short briefing, they kept hopeful eyes on Hagerty, waiting for their coach to tell them what was going on and how they should react to the unfamiliar situation. Hagerty faced them, shrugged, and answered their unspoken question.

"You know as much about it as I do," he said frankly. "I only know, or rather I only hope, that a big change of some sort has taken place, and I hope the change is for the better. There is no way for me to know how far the cat will jump, or in what direction. I'd be guessing, and if I guessed wrong it might only foul you up. We've got to play this one by ear, and your ears are as good as mine. Just do the best you can."

The Pelicans had an early chance to use their ears. The band, as usual, formed in two lines at the entrance to the field, leaving a lane through which the Pelicans would make their entrance. Ding Kibby, as captain, led his teammates as they ran upon the field. Andy was close enough to the front to see that Ding almost stumbled as he jogged into the open and was hit by a solid wave of sound.

It caught the other Pelicans as they emerged. The line wavered, rallied, and kept moving, a file of confused football players trying to adjust themselves to something they had not experienced since the season started. They were not geared to it.

Andy felt the shock. He wondered, with a touch of worry, what effect it might have on the Pelicans as well as himself. Would it bring them to their peak or would it impose an added burden as they tried to prove that they deserved this welcome? Even more disturbing was the thought that this opening ovation, though spontaneous, might be a mere flash in the pan. Would the fans feel that, by this loud welcome, they had made up for their past neglect? When the game got under way, would they return to their past indifference if the Pelicans did not perform according to their expectations or demands? They were questions Andy could not answer.

He was, nevertheless, unable to quench a persistent spark of optimism. He could not shrug off the present demonstration. These fans did not appear to be hysterically insistent that their team get busy and perform a miracle. Andy believed he sensed a deeper substance to the noise, the determination to claim ownership of a personal possession, something they had almost lost through carelessness.

CHAPTER

18

Coach Hagerty had also listened to the fans. It may have influenced his last minute decision to put Mark Sutton in the starting line-up. It was a gamble, but a wise gamble if it worked. Mark, throughout the season, had proved himself to be the best man for the spot, and Hagerty needed his best man against the powerful Marlins. He was gambling that the Pelicans, involved in their new relationship with the fans, would once more accept Mark as a teammate.

Andy, watching critically, saw no resentment in the Pelicans when Hagerty announced his choice. They were still in a mild fog as the fans continued to encourage them. Mark, on the other hand, was virtually pathetic in his gratitude. His morale for the past week had been low. He had not expected to play against the Marlins. He could not conceal a feverish haste to prove himself, to regain the esteem of the Pelicans.

Ding Kibby joined the officials and the Marlin captain, Tug Brady, in the center of the field for the toss of the coin. The referee flipped the coin, then went through the elaborate pantomime which informed the bleachers that the Marlins had won the toss and had elected to receive. Tug Brady gave Ding what appeared to be a patronizing handshake, and the two captains returned to their squads.

The usual expectant silence settled on the crowd when the teams moved into position for the kickoff. Ralph Hopper booted a long one to the Marlin five-yard line. He had tried to keep the kick off-center to avoid the Marlin speedster, Jake Faber. The kickoff, unfortunately, went right down the slot and Faber pulled it in. He waited for his blockers to get out ahead, then set sail for Pelican territory.

The Pelicans, however, were not loafing. They came down fast under the kick, and, even though they appeared to scramble more than necessary, they managed to prevent Faber from staging one of his fantastic runbacks. They piled the play up on the twenty-six-yard line. The Pelican cheering section showed approval.

The Marlins exploded from the huddle with the eager air of men who could scarcely wait to get their teeth into a tasty meal. Their haste, however, did not disrupt their co-ordination. The play got under way with smooth precision. Andy sensed something frighteningly mechanical in the way the Marlins moved, as each man performed his task with an exactness which ignored all possibility of error. The play went wide. The blocking was deadly. Jake Faber, carrying the ball, was forced out of bounds after a fourteen-yard gain.

Andy watched the play without enjoyment, knowing that, if this opening play was a true picture of Marlin football, he was seeing a great team in action, a team which certainly deserved its formidable reputation. He could only hope that plays to follow would not display such co-ordinated power.

He received small encouragement on the next play. The Marlin quarterback, Cliff Dane, drew in the Pelican line-backers with a fake line plunge, then flipped a short pass over the center of the line. His right end, Hap Hatcher, pulled it in for a twelve-yard gain.

Andy, trying not to be too critical, realized that the play, although well executed, might easily have been broken up. Mark Sutton could have batted down that pass. It was completed in his defense area, but Mark, too eager to back up a line play, had allowed himself to be fooled. He shot a worried glance toward the bench, displaying the guilt he probably felt.

When the Marlins went back into their huddle, Andy got a brief impression that he chose to believe was hopeful. The Marlins, in two plays, had advanced the ball into Pelican territory on the forty-eight-yard line. They had done so without apparent effort, and, as they bent into their huddle, Andy believed he detected a slight letdown, a slackening of tautness. They acted like men who had confirmed something to their satisfaction, something they had suspected all along— that the Pelicans were, indeed, pushovers.

When the Marlins came from the huddle, this attitude seemed more marked than ever. Andy kept his fingers crossed, well aware of the effect that overconfidence can have upon a team. He waited for the effect to show, and he waited vainly. Tug Brady blasted through the center of the line for seven yards. Brady then picked up a first down through the same spot, and Andy sadly tossed his theory down the drain. If the Marlins were overconfident, it obviously did not affect their game. Their play was automatic and instinctive.

Andy sat and sweated miserably as he watched his team get pushed around. The Marlins undoubtedly were good, but Andy was doggedly convinced that the Pelicans were not as bad as they appeared to be. They definitely were not clicking properly, yet while he sat there suffering, he could not help but listen to the fans. And then it hit him suddenly that the Pelicans also were probably keeping their ears tuned to the rooters despite their efforts to keep their minds on football. It could account, to a large extent, for the brand of football they were playing.

The Pelicans, to start with, were hearing something they had not heard all season, sincere encouragement from the bleachers. Instead of bolstering their game, it was confusing them, because they were afraid to believe that the encouragement could last long under these conditions. They were trying hard, of course, to better the conditions. Meanwhile, they were listening involuntarily for a change of tone or for the indifferent silence to which they were accustomed.

The Marlins, whether or not they recognized it, took prompt advantage of the Pelicans' condition. With first down on the Pelican thirty-seven-yard line they shook Jake Faber loose on a screen pass. He went all the way behind hard-hitting interference. Mark Sutton had a chance to bounce him out of bounds on the ten-yard line, but Faber outfoxed him with change of pace. Faber sailed across the goal line while Mark climbed from the ground in a bewildered sort of way. The Marlins rubbed things in by going for the two-point conversion. They made it good with a cutback through the line. The score was 8-0.

The Pelicans deployed to receive the kickoff, shifting nervously on their feet. The fans continued to encourage them and, so far as Andy could tell, the noise was just as loud as ever. Some of the Pelicans still seemed doubtful, but Andy saw others draw in a few deep breaths as if telling themselves, "It's too good to last, but we might as well make the best of it while it does last."

The kickoff came to Mark. He grabbed it like a hungry chicken capturing a bug and then got under way as if afraid someone would take it from him. His interference formed, but Mark barged into it in wild-eyed haste. The Marlins downed him on the fourteen-yard line.

Ding called for a fake line buck by Ralph Hopper on the first down. The ball was to go to the left half, Ken Bush, on a delayed hand-off, and Bush, with good speed, was supposed to sweep around the end. The play might have gained some ground if Mark Sutton had not missed a block. The man to whom he was assigned snaked through to nail Bush for a two-yard loss. Ding called time out to talk things over with Mark, and Hagerty took prompt advantage of the moment. He sent Joe Jasper in to replace Mark Sutton.

Mark came slowly off the field. Andy half expected him to blow his top when he reached Hagerty, but Mark was a beaten man. He slumped dejectedly on the bench, and Andy came close to feeling sorry for him. He compromised by holding the charitable thought that Mark might have learned an important lesson. If Mark made an honest effort to redeem himself during his next two years in school, he might turn out to be a good guy after all.

Ding had little choice at this time other than to keep the ball on the ground. It was too early in the game and the Pelicans were too deep in their own territory to risk anything fancy against a team like the Marlins. On the second down Ralph Hopper had a try at the Marlin line and found it pretty solid. He got through for three yards and that was all.

The Pelicans quick-kicked on the third down. The play started from a straight T, with Ralph in the center spot. He faded a few steps and took a direct snap from Sam at center when Ding stepped from the line of the ball. Ralph caught the Marlins napping. The ball landed behind the Marlin safety man and took a Pelican roll. The Marlins downed it on their own thirty-two-yard line.

The Marlins put their juggernaut in motion once again. They carved out five yards on the first line play and six yards on the next one. The reason was obvious enough. The Marlin forward wall was getting a split-second jump on the Pelican linemen, the split second which could make a tremendous difference in defense or offense, because the man who makes first contact in line play usually comes out the winner.

The relentless march continued into Pelican territory, yet the Pelican fans kept on with their encouragement. Andy wondered, as his teammates must be wondering, when the breaking point would come. Andy was almost guilty of wishing it would come soon, in which event the Pelicans would at least know where they stood.

Ding broke up a long pass which probably would have gone for a touchdown. It left the Marlins with a third and four situation on the Pelican twenty-eight-yard line. The next play might have been a pass, a screen, or an end sweep, but it had no chance to develop. Sam Tedder blitzed the quarterback, Cliff Dane. Sam crashed his way into the Marlin backfield, and, with his deceptive knack of moving fast for a short distance, smothered Dane with a high tackle before Dane could get rid of the ball. The play went for a twelve-yard loss, the first break the Pelicans had had.

The Marlins kicked on the fourth down, missing the side line and sending the ball across the goal line for a touchback. When the ball was brought out twenty yards and put in play, Andy was mildly optimistic, hoping that Sam's performance might have put new life into the Pelicans. It looked that way for a little while. They managed to scratch out a first down, but the attack bogged on the second series of plays. The Pelicans had to kick.

The Marlins went on the attack again, a methodical grinding out of yardage. Their overhead attack was sound and dangerous, yet they seemed to prefer hammering out their gains in a show of power, because it emphasized the difference between a fine team and a mediocre one. They proved their point. The Pelicans looked definitely mediocre against the Marlins' smooth, co-ordinated power. They made their advance look as insulting as they could, the picture of a grown man pushing a small boy aside.

The Pelican fans still yelled encouragement. Andy was reasonably sure that the yells were losing some of their force, and it seemed a mere question of time before the fans would run entirely out of steam.

The Marlins cheated themselves of another touchdown by a pair of penalties back to back, a roughing penalty and a man-in-motion penalty. The twenty-yard handicap forced a kick. The Pelicans went on the attack again, or what they chose to believe was an attack. The Marlins, obviously peeved at their setback, showed their teeth and stopped the home team in its tracks. Then, still annoyed at themselves, they set out to prove that they could score a touchdown any time they wanted to. They mixed a few ground plays with an aerial attack.

They crossed the goal line as the gun went off to end the quarter. They converted for another two points, and the score was 16-0.

This, thought Andy dismally, is the end. It's got to be. The Pelicans on the field may have been holding the same thought, yet they tried hard not to show it as they plodded grimly toward positions to receive the kickoff. Andy decided sadly that the fans were thinking, "What's the use? We tried." He turned his head to face the silent stands and his interest quickened. They were paying close attention to the head cheer leader, who had his big megaphone trained on them. He tossed the megaphone aside and raised his arms. And then it happened.

It was a long cheer and a corny cheer, as most cheers are. It ended with the conventional, "Fight, team, fight!" but never before had Andy heard a cheer quite like the one that surged around him now. The words were unimportant. It was the quality of sound that made the difference. He felt goose pimples rising on his skin. He tried to warn himself that his imagination was playing tricks on him. He could not, however, go against the evidence of his own eyes, because if his imagination was at fault the Pelicans on the field were in the same boat.

They came to a dead stop, every one of them. They turned to face their fans as if pulled around with strings. They stood for several seconds, staring with disbelief. Then, one by one, they shook themselves from the momentary trance. They began to walk again, exchanging glances as if asking one another, "Did you hear it too? Or am I the only one who's nuts?"

When nothing but the echoes of the cheer remained, Andy sat in frowning thought. These fans had had nothing to cheer about all season. They had nothing tangible to cheer about right now, yet they had put their hearts into this effort. They may have been offering their very best apology for things they had left undone. They may have been trying to tell the Pelicans, "You've shown us you've got guts. It's time we showed you we've got some."

Andy's speculations left unanswered questions. How would it affect the team? How long would the effect last? He centered his attention on the men, and what he saw encouraged him. They were firmly planted as they waited for the kickoff. There was no uncertain shifting of their feet as if their minds were not entirely upon football.

Andy could only guess what they were thinking, and his guess was ruled by the things that *he* would think if he were out there. He would think he had misjudged the fans, their tenacity, their guts, and their desire to make things right. He might think they were behind him now right up to the end. They had had their chance to quit. They had watched the Marlins score two easy touchdowns without much opposition, yet they had served loud notice they were still behind the Pelicans. The message they had sent could mean, at worst, that they could watch their boys lose a football game without loud criticism while the game was going on. This, in itself, was a long step in the right direction. These were the thoughts that Andy held. He still wondered what the men out there were thinking, and how it would affect their game.

He soon found out. The change was not spectacular or abrupt, but it was there and it was growing. The Pelicans were facing an unfamiliar situation that required adjustment, and they seemed to realize that the game was relatively young, that an adjustment of this sort was nothing to be rushed.

Early indications of the change were evidenced by new alertness in the men. With nothing to sidetrack their thoughts their concentration was improving. They were able now to think about football and nothing else. For the first time in the game they could give the Marlins their undivided attention. They could recall more clearly the things they had learned about the Marlins from the blackboard and the movie sessions, and the Pelicans were gradually applying these things to their own use.

The improvement in the Pelicans was gradual enough to cause the visitors no immediate alarm. The Marlins could easily assume that the Pelicans had been temporarily overawed by the Marlins' reputation and that the Pelicans were now settling down to their normal game which, though slightly better than the Marlins had anticipated, was nothing to cause them much concern.

The most significant development, as Andy saw it,

was the increasing strength of the Pelican defense. They were no longer being pushed around like a herd of bewildered sheep. The forward wall was charging faster, and the line-backers showed up in unexpected places, spots where they were needed most. Andy recognized this as an encouraging sign, knowing that a team with confidence in its defense is bound to have more confidence in its offense.

The Pelican offense was also showing gradual improvement. There was nothing spectacular about it, no long gains. The Pelicans hacked out occasional first downs, going about it in the manner of men who were conducting an experiment, and who wanted to be sure they were on the right track before allowing themselves to get too optimistic.

An impartial critic, at this stage of the game, would have to choose the Marlins as the better team on the field. They gained more ground on the attack and were more impressive on defense. It could not be overlooked, however, that their gains did not carry them across the goal line, a matter which began to cause the Marlins some annoyance as the half drew toward its close. They stepped up their efforts in a hasty way, which indicated they were puzzled, not sure of what was happening. The haste did not improve their game.

The Pelicans, on the other hand, offered no great threat to the Marlin goal line, even though they advanced the ball on two occasions into Marlin territory, a big improvement over their first-period efforts. The Pelicans were not offering their fans much reason for excited cheering. It was more important that the fans were offered no further reason for discouragement, and, once they had accepted this, the yells took on a slowly rising note of hope, a change of tone which was not wasted on the Pelicans.

The ball was in their possession in the closing minutes of the half. It was not a passing situation, with the ball deep in their own territory, so Ding wisely chose to keep his plays upon the ground. He sent Joe Jasper around left end, and Ken Bush, a dependable blocking back, fulfilled his assignment by wiping out the Marlin end with a savage block. Bush opened up a six-yard gain for Jasper, but Bush stayed on the ground. Ding called time out, and the trainer hurried on the field.

Hagerty called sharply, "Okay, Andy, on your feet!"

Andy's breath jammed in his throat as he came off the bench. He had hoped for a chance to play against the Marlins, but not until this moment did he fully understand what such a chance might mean. He was briefly sorry that it had to happen at the expense of another man, but there was no time now for such regrets. He started on the field as Bush, with a rib injury, was being helped to the side line.

As Andy jogged toward the Pelicans, buckling his helmet, his thoughts were in a tangled mess. He was not worried about the technical aspects of playing left half instead of right half, because Hagerty, with his limited material, had taken great pains to make his backfield interchangeable.

Andy's big problem at the moment was to forget his

previous trips upon the field in the role of substitute. At these times he had been plagued with the great urgency to prove himself, to establish himself as someone more important than Jocko Baker's son. Always in the past he had entered the game with the worried feeling that this was his big chance, and that it might be his last chance. He had been harassed in the past with the conviction that he had some fine football in his system, yet some mysterious restricting elements had always prevented it from coming to the surface.

Despite his efforts to subdue it, the breathless urgency was still with him, and he knew that if it stayed with him he would be no more impressive on the gridiron than he had been in the past. There was one hope left—probably a feeble one—the Pelicans themselves. He had watched their gradual transformation. He had tried to feel what they were feeling, yet not until he joined them was the full impact of their change brought home to him.

He had moved, at other times, into a team of grimly desperate men. The grimness was still there, but Andy found no trace of desperation. The quality he found was hard to analyze. The Pelicans welcomed him with no enthusiasm and with no resentment. They glanced at him like men with other things upon their minds, in the manner of scientists perhaps, who, on the brink of a great discovery, refuse to have their concentration interrupted by a visitor.

Andy had the strange impression that the Pelicans were enveloped by some sort of aura that protected them from everything outside their own tight world. When he moved into the huddle he could feel the intangible thing close protectively about him. It was almost frightening at first. These men were virtually strangers. It was hard to believe he had been in a huddle with these same men on previous occasions.

The time remaining in the second period was too short for Andy to determine how these new conditions might affect his game. Ding, giving Andy a chance to adjust himself, assigned him a minor role in the next two plays, which carved out a first down. The gun went off before the Pelicans could keep their attack moving. They were a sober, thoughtful group of men as they headed for the dressing room.

CHAPTER
19

THE mood was still upon the Pelicans when they reached the dressing room. They remained strangely silent, unwilling to discuss the portion of the game behind them or the portion still ahead. They seemed to prefer the solitude of their own thoughts, as if any nonessential conversation at this stage might break a spell they wanted to preserve.

Hagerty was wise enough to sense that no intrusion at this point was necessary. He moved quietly among them, making himself available and letting them know by the manner of his bearing that he was thoroughly satisfied, that he had no criticisms or suggestions. The trainer, catching the idea, worked silently on minor injuries.

Andy started to absorb the feeling all about him, not knowing exactly what it was, but glad to find himself receptive to it. It began to work inside him like fermenting yeast, bringing with it an odd quality of excitement which affected him like tonic. He clung to the feeling as the Pelicans started for the field. He guarded it jealously as if fearful that it might desert him.

He need not have worried. The warm greeting of the fans made it more secure. It was still there when the Pelicans deployed to receive the kickoff, a peculiar tingling unlike anything he had known before. Even so, he was not rash enough to hope the kick would come to him. He did not believe he was quite ready for so much responsibility.

He had no choice. The kick came tumbling in his direction. He yanked in a quick breath, which scarcely passed the tightness of his throat. Ding's calm voice said, "Easy does it," and the tightness passed. The object coming toward him looked like an ordinary football now instead of like some hurtling projectile. He judged it carefully, and when it reached his hands they eased it back against his body.

He fought against the sudden impulse to uncork all the speed he had. He got prompt help from another voice, unhurried yet impelling, "Let's go, Andy!" It reminded him that he was not alone, that the responsibility was not entirely his, that others were on hand to share it. He checked his first two hasty strides and watched the men ahead of him.

It was a sight to instill confidence in a ball carrier. The Pelicans moved fast, yet with a deadly purpose out of keeping with their desperate, frantic blocking efforts of the past. They picked their men instead of hurling their bodies at the first available opponent. They timed their blocks with a neat precision Andy had not seen in them before.

The demonstration of smooth teamwork had a quick effect on Andy, even though he had no time to understand exactly what was happening. He merely had the vague impression that these men ahead of him were generating a fantastic force which swept Andy with it. He found himself performing things which seemed entirely unconnected with his brain, a side step here, a lightning swerve a few steps farther on, following an instinct which came out of nowhere. It seemed almost as if the men ahead were thinking for him, or else his own thoughts had suddenly become meshed with theirs.

His runback carried him to the forty-two-yard line. When he came from underneath the pile of Marlins he expected to find an exuberant bunch of Pelicans, but all the exuberance, and there was plenty of it, came from the fans. The Pelicans themselves were still deep in their well of concentration. They moved fast, yet they moved with purpose, behaving like men who were not surprised at Andy's runback, but who merely considered it as something to be repeated. The Marlins were not noticeably upset, choosing probably to regard the runback as a fluke, the kind of thing that happens now and then to any team.

The Pelicans went on the attack. Andy could feel vibrations in the huddle. Ding must have felt them too. He called his play with the air of a man who has decided to quit fooling around and shoot the works. He

called for a long side-line pass for which the timing
had to be exactly perfect.

The play got under way. Both ends and Andy went
downfield as possible receivers. The Pelican line held
like a stone wall, giving Ding time enough to write a
letter home. The Marlins may have been taken by
surprise. Their pass defense was not as effective as it
should have been. Andy, on the other hand, deserved
considerable credit for his part in the play.

He sprinted down the middle of the field and, finding
himself well covered by the Marlin safety man, was
certain Ding would not pick him for a target. Interference had wiped out a couple of potential pass defenders,
and when Andy saw Jake Faber on his way to cover the
Pelican right end, Jay Seever, he suddenly cut back
with a buttonhook which cleared him of the safety man
and made it look as if a buttonhook pass was what the
play had called for.

Faber got the idea fast. He hesitated briefly as if uncertain whether to cover Andy or Seever, and that short
hesitation was the break Ding Kibby needed. He rifled
the ball to Seever, scoring a bull's-eye. The play went
for twenty-eight yards to place the ball on the Marlin
thirty-yard line.

The Marlins, visibly shaken by this sudden turn of
the tide, dug in with a show of anger. Ding split his
ends and moved Andy to a wing-back spot, where he
could get a fast start downfield as a possible pass receiver. The Marlins, logically assuming that the Peli-

cans might push their luck with another pass, promptly loosened their defense. Ding, just as promptly, went through on a quarterback sneak while Sam bulldozed a path for him. The surprise play was good for nine yards, bringing the Pelicans to the twenty-one-yard line.

The Marlins called time out to regroup their forces. A substitute ran in with obvious instructions from the bench. When time was called in, the Marlins were ready for anything, recognizing it as a fine spot for a pass play, because, if the pass failed, the Pelicans would still have two more chances to make the first down.

Ding accommodated them with a pass, but not of the touchdown variety. He faked Hopper into the line, then flipped a lateral to Andy, who waited with nice timing until the screen had formed ahead of him. The screen put on another show of deadly blocking. They cleared a path for Andy into the Marlin backfield, where suddenly it seemed that Marlins were closing in from all directions. Andy had no time to think or to choose a course of action. He seemed to be moving in some sort of violent dream with no control over his arms or legs. They did the things *they* wanted to, controlled by some deep instinct that had waited long to be released.

He felt the jar of hands against his legs as if the legs belonged to someone else. His arm, if it actually belonged to him, flashed out in savage straight-arms against hard helmets. He finally felt the crashing impact of a tackle he could not avoid. He managed a last forward lunge and hit the ground with a force that cleared his mind. He stared with unbelieving eyes at the broad white stripe beneath his body. The ball was safely in the end zone.

The attempt at a two-point conversion failed, a failure which appeared to make no difference to the fans. As the Pelicans marched grimly up the field they leaned against a wall of sound. Andy found himself walking beside Sam.

"I think we can lick these guys," said Sam. "I don't know why I think so, but I do. How do you feel about it?"

"I don't know how I feel," admitted Andy, "because I've never felt this way before. Everything is different."

"I know," said Sam. "I'll bet you don't even know how you scored that touchdown."

"It seemed as if someone else was doing it," said Andy.

Sam nodded. "I'm charging that line faster than I ever did before. It's just as if someone were pushing me. I know it sounds crazy, but I think the fans are doing it."

Andy did not bother to dispute this, because he had a strong hunch that Sam was hitting close to the truth. It was too early yet for Andy to be entirely sure. He had to assume, in order to be sensible, that the Pelicans' last surge might have been a temporary thing which would not be repeated, even with the fans' assistance.

Andy's doubts, in this respect, were soon dispelled as the game got under way again. The Pelicans, miraculously, appeared to be getting stronger. They were playing the sort of football they had been taught to play, but they were playing it with uncluttered minds, which permitted all the things they had learned to remain uppermost.

They were playing the Marlins, at this stage, on even terms in a crazy upset of all pre-game dope. More crazy still was the bald fact that their game continued to increase in power, a miracle for which Andy finally had to give the fans full credit.

Their cheering, satisfactory before, was now dynamic. It had taken on a new and penetrating tone. To this point it had been dutiful and courageous. They had yelled encouragement because they felt they owed it to the team. This was different, a whole lot different. It suddenly hit them with the force of a blackjack that the Pelicans actually had a chance to win. The fans had tasted blood and they wanted more. Their yells took on a thundering overtone of sheer pride.

The yells were penetrating. Andy could feel them spreading through his system like a hypodermic injection. He could feel the stimulating boost, and he knew the other Pelicans were having the same reaction. For the first time this season they were trying to give the fans what they wanted, because the fans were demanding it in the proper way.

There was no further scoring in the third period, even though the Marlins made a powerful effort to regain the initiative, an effort which came dangerously close to paying off. They started a drive which had the earmarks of a full-scale invasion. It was a seasoned team not easily discouraged by strong opposition. They proved it now. They settled down to their best game of football. They uncorked their full bag of tricks. They threw in everything they had.

They were double-teaming on Sam Tedder now, assigning a pair of men to neutralize Sam's strength. It placed an added burden on the Pelican line-backers. Andy had always considered line-backing one of his main weaknesses, because he could be easily fooled, yet now he was anticipating plays, and for the most part he was guessing right. The reason was not clear except that his football instinct, long restricted, was now working at full speed. His sharp tackling and pass protection had helped a lot to keep the Marlins from scoring sooner in the offensive they were staging.

The Pelicans, in past games, could not have slowed the drive as they were doing now. They refused to panic, refused to abandon the new confidence they had found and that their fans continued to pour into them. They stalled the Marlins, fourth down six to go, on the eighteen-yard line. The Marlins sent in their field-goal specialist, apparently willing to settle for three points.

When the ball was snapped from center, Andy did something he had not planned to do at all. It could have been pure hunch or football instinct, but instead of joining the charge to block the kick, he whirled and started for the goal line. It was a lucky or a brilliant move, because the place kick was a fake. The quarter-back received the ball, jumped up, and whipped it to an end who was already in the end zone waiting for the pass. It almost reached him, but not quite. Andy, timing his long lunge, made it good. His hand slapped solidly against the ball and drove it to the ground. The ball was given to the Pelicans on their twenty-yard line. They went to work again.

When the Pelicans started grinding out the yardage, something began to happen to the Marlins. It was hardly noticeable at first, but a team as highly tuned as the Pelicans was quick to sense it. The Marlins were letting down. The Marlins were not gutless. The Marlins were not quitters, they were only human.

They were seasoned football players, who had learned to cope with any normal situation they encountered. The situation they encountered now, however, was not normal. It was unreasonable, insane. They had expected to meet a weak team in the Pelicans, and even though the Pelicans had shown an unexpected strength the Marlins could have geared themselves to meet it.

The thing no team could possibly be prepared to meet was a team whose strength uncannily increased as play continued. It was something to defy all reason, and the Marlins gradually began to act as if they were facing men from outer space, eleven men who drove relentlessly ahead with no regard for human patterns of behavior.

The Marlins began to show the first signs of panic. They called time out more frequently. Their strong reserves came rushing in only to catch the nervous jitters from the men already in the game. The Marlins finally showed the full extent of their frustration. Accepting Ding Kibby as the Pelican leader and the man most valuable to the team, they ganged up on him. It was a crude and clumsy foul. They hit him an instant after he had released a pass. They dislocated Ding's right knee, then accepted the long penalty with the satisfied air of men who had eliminated a major threat.

Their satisfaction was premature. They had not counted on the Pelicans' sizzling anger, nor on the speed of Ding's replacement, Jerry Holt. The Pelicans had the ball, third down four to go, on their own forty-three-yard line. Jerry brought the signal in from Hagerty—a fake pass and a keeper.

The Pelicans contained their wrath until the play got under way, then they cut loose. Their blocks were sharp and vicious. Jerry swung wide, faked a running pass, then tucked the ball beneath his arm and headed for pay dirt. The Pelicans mowed a wide path for him. Faber, the Marlin speedster might have had a chance to get across in time, but Andy got there first. He jolted Faber off balance with a shoulder block. Andy kept his feet, and moved in to protect Jerry from behind. It was wasted effort, because Jerry, once in the clear, needed no protection. He streaked across the goal line all alone. The Pelicans tried for another two-point conversion, but once again their luck was bad. The score was 16-12.

The Marlins tried to start another strong attack. The Pelicans had a different idea on the matter. The Marlins squeezed out one first down following the kickoff, after which the Pelican defense forced them to punt. The third quarter ended before the Pelicans could get under way. The teams changed goals and the Pelicans began to move again, with Jerry doing an excellent job as Ding's replacement.

The Marlins put up a desperate, last-ditch stand after the Pelicans had hammered their way to the Marlin twenty-two-yard line, first down. The Marlins, making no bones about it, were playing defensive football, trying to protect their four-point lead. They knocked down an attempted pass. They held a line play to four yards, leaving the Pelicans in a three and six situation.

Jerry called an end-zone pass, a rather obvious play which the Marlins might expect except for the sad lesson they had learned concerning Jerry's speed. They could always assume that Jerry, accepting the option, might make a run for it. They had to watch for it and keep him covered.

Andy got a fast start from his wing spot when the ball was snapped. He headed for the goal posts, noting promptly that Jake Faber had decided to keep him covered. Andy held his course through the middle of the posts. Once in the end zone, he faked a quick stride to the right, then, on his next stride, cut sharply to the left, leaving Faber stranded.

The pass would come to the deep left corner of the end zone if Jerry picked Andy as a receiver. Andy shot a glance across his shoulder. He grunted with alarm when he saw the pigskin coming toward him. The alarm was genuine, because the pass was not leading the receiver far enough. Andy came to a jolting stop, knowing that Faber would have time to get there too.

Andy's fear was justified. Faber and the ball arrived together. Both men went into the air. Andy was certain he had never jumped so high before, and his jump, by an inch or so, turned out to be the better of the two. He felt the ball slap hard against his hands. There was an agonizing instant when the ball, like something active and alive, was trying to squirm from his fingers. He was never quite sure how he subdued it, but when he hit the ground in a tangle with Jake Faber, the ball was hugged securely against Andy's chest. Ralph Hopper kicked the extra point to make the score 19-16 with the Pelicans on the long end.

The Pelican fans went into hysterics. The Marlin fans sat stunned and silent. The Marlins went to pieces. Their only choice was to take wild chances through the air. Andy intercepted one of these desperation passes. He almost went the distance with Jerry as a convoy. When a Marlin came in for the tackle, Andy managed to get rid of the ball before he hit the ground. He flipped it back to Jerry Holt, who scampered over for his second touchdown.

The Pelicans were tired, a weary, battered group of men, but they had something left, enough to keep the Marlins from another score. When the game was over, the Pelicans might have found the strength to walk off the field. They had no chance to prove it. The Pelicans, and Hagerty as well, were carried from the field on the shoulders of the wild-eyed fans. Walking would have been more comfortable, but not as pleasant.

The celebration in the dressing room was something to behold. The Pelicans were no longer sober, thoughtful men. They were hilarious kids.

When the excitement had subsided somewhat, Sam asked Andy, "Have you got plans for this evening?"

"Yes, I'm having dinner with my father." The words came out in an unenthusiastic way that didn't sound quite right to Andy. He wondered why, and suddenly it occurred to him. "I think I'm going to enjoy it," he said.